A LOVE SO Deep

To The Bone
Book Three

By Lili Valente

A LOVE SO Deep

By Lili Valente

Self Taught Ninja Press

About the Book

Warning: Hold on tight for the red hot, adrenaline fueled conclusion to the To the Bone series.

What we have is sacred, a bond forged by pain and pleasure, suffering and passion, and Gabe is right—nothing will tear us apart again. This is forever, for keeps, for the rest of our lives, no matter what the future holds.

We just have to outsmart the powerful people determined to keep us apart.

I'm prepared to fight our enemies, but I'm not prepared for *him*. For a monster wearing a friendly face, or the nightmare he's determined to unleash.

They say it's better to have loved and lost than never to have loved at all. I say—over my dead body. They'll have to pry forever out of my cold, clawed hands.

A Love So Deep is the final book in the To the Bone series.

"And softness came from the starlight
and filled me full to the bone."
–W.B. Yeats

CHAPTER
one

Gabe

*"Tis in my memory lock'd,
And you yourself shall keep the key of it."*
-Shakespeare

Before I was diagnosed with an allegedly inoperable brain tumor and nearly died, I had no interest in the obituary page.

I was young and immortal. I was going to live forever, go out in a blaze of glory, and I couldn't care less how many unlucky people had the misfortune to die on a given week.

After the surgery, I read the Giffney

Gazette's obituary page every Sunday morning, thumbing through the snapshots of lives lost as I linger over my coffee. It was only luck that kept me from gracing these pages. I feel obligated to read every entry, like I owe it to the people less fortunate than myself to read about the children and grandchildren they left behind, and the many adventures they had before they got old and set in their ways and hunkered down to waste the rest of their lives watching television.

But until today, I haven't known any of the recently deceased personally.

When I read that Charles Edwin Cooney has died at age fifty-four, leaving behind five children, and one grandchild, I can't say that I'm sad, but I feel the news. It hits me physically, tightening my throat, making my stomach clench around my second cup of coffee.

Chuck is dead, and one more avenue to finding Caitlin is closed forever.

Not like you've been looking too hard lately, anyway.

"What's wrong, dear?" My mother leans across the table, peering into my face, as attuned to my moods now as she has been since the moment I came out of surgery.

I don't remember my mother being this

concerned about my emotional well-being last summer—or any of the twenty years before—but Deborah is clearly trying to make the most of our second chance. She's determined to be the plugged-in parent she never was when I was growing up, no matter how irritating I find it, or how uncomfortable and strange this forced intimacy is for the both of us.

"I'm fine," I say, folding my paper in half. "Just read that Charles Cooney died."

I watch her face as she reacts, but her eyes are cool and unreadable, the way they always are when the Cooney name comes up in conversation. "Well, that's sad."

"It is," I say. "He was in his early fifties."

"That's what hard living will do to a person," my dad offers, not looking up from his own section of the paper, apparently unmoved by the news that my ex-girlfriend's father is dead.

According to my parents, they didn't know Caitlin and I were dating last summer. I kept our relationship a secret from them, and they have no clue what happened to her, or why we ended things. They're very convincing, but I know they're lying. I remember sitting next to Caitlin at this very table, running my hand up and down the silky soft skin of her thigh, thinking about all the things I wanted to do to her as soon as we were free of my parents.

But Deborah and Aaron don't know I'm recovering my memories.

Or that I *was* recovering them.

Since the night I saw Caitlin with the bruises on her throat, I've done my best to let sleeping demons lie. I keep my thoughts in the present, and steer clear of places that remind me of Caitlin. I take a sleeping pill before I go to bed, and I fuck Kimmy with a certain degree of reserve, not wanting to lose control and swing too close to the edge of the chasm. I don't want to glimpse the skeletons I sense are littering the ground on the other side. I'm afraid I'll learn something about myself that will make the surgery, and all the days I've fought to recover, pointless.

If I killed her, I don't deserve to be alive.

If I killed her, there is only one course of action I can take, and that would certainly be a waste, though I hear a good number of people like me do commit suicide. The post-operative fog, the feelings of alienation, and the sense that you will never be the person you were before—the person everyone in your life wants you to be so badly—is too much for a lot of people. They would rather check out, letting a bullet finish the job the tumor started.

"You won't go to the funeral will you?" Deborah asks, breaking into my thoughts.

I shake my head. "Why would I?"

Deborah looks flustered, but only for a second. By the time she speaks, her cool has returned. "Of course not. Don't know what I was thinking." She smiles. "What about church? Are you joining us this morning? Might lift your spirits."

"My spirits are fine," I say, forcing a smile. "And I think I'd rather worship in my own way today. I'll probably take a ride, and meet you for lunch after."

My father chuckles. "I wish I could get away with worshiping in my own way."

"Your brand of worship involves way too much time on a fishing boat," my mother says, taking another sip of her coffee. "You're only home two days a week as it is. I'm not going to give up an entire day to the catfish in Lake Anderson."

"You could go with him," I suggest, though it's hard to imagine my perfectly pulled together mother baking in the sun on a fishing boat.

Deborah raises one thin, blond brow. The dubious expression on her face makes me smile. Sometimes I like Deborah, even if she is a manipulative liar. Considering my own, checkered history, I'm not really in any position to judge.

"Sorry, must have been the tumor hole talking." I stand and circle the table, leaning down to kiss her cheek. "See you at noon."

"We're going to Peabody's on the square," Deborah says, patting my arm. "The Jamisons are coming, and I've only got reservations for six, so don't bring a guest."

I clench my jaw, biting back the smartass remark on the tip of my tongue. I know which "guest" Deborah is talking about, but there's no point in getting into an argument about Kimmy. If Kimmy and I hadn't run into my mother at the grocery store last week, Deborah never would have met my latest fling.

Kimmy and I are fuck buddies, nothing more. I don't plan on keeping in touch after I leave for school, and Kimmy doesn't even know how long she'll be in town. She has a six-month lease, and a job as a cocktail waitress, but no real ties to Giffney. This is just the place she ended up when her money for bus fare ran out. She has dreams of moving home to Louisiana and opening a fabric store, and I have dreams of going back to the university, picking up where I left off, and pretending this long, strange detour never happened.

Or at least that's one of the lies I tell myself.

What I really want is something very different.

What I want is for this hole inside of me to be filled up with something. Someone. I want to know Caitlin wasn't a dream, and that I'm not a monster.

And so, when I hear my parents' car pull down the driveway on their way to church, I don't go to the barn to saddle my horse. I head down to the Beamer and drive into town, across the railroad tracks, to the ranch house where Caitlin used to live.

A LOVE SO DEEP

CHAPTER
Two

Gabe

I pull slowly around the cul-de-sac and park behind a silver Toyota Camry I don't recognize from similar drive-bys. It's an older car, but in good condition, with Florida plates and a bumper sticker that reads "Progress not Perfection." The driver's side door opens and a feminine foot wearing a shiny white sandal emerges.

Not wanting to get caught spying on the Cooney house, I'm about to start the car and pull away, when the rest of the woman emerges, and the world tilts on its axis.

I'm certain that it's her—Caitlin Cooney, alive and well. The long blond hair is the same shade of honey and caramel, and the slim build achingly familiar. For a moment, relief floods through my body, turning my insides to liquid, but then the woman turns, and my hope goes swirling down the drain.

The hair is the same, but this woman is taller, with an oval face instead of the heart-shaped one I was expecting. She is beautiful, but she isn't Caitlin, and judging by the wedding ring on her finger and the baby bump beneath her flowered sundress, she's not a candidate for my Summer of Blondes, either.

Still, as she turns to look at the Cooney house, there is something in the slope of her nose that is so familiar I feel compelled to learn who she is.

I pull the keys from the ignition and step out of the car. When my door slams, the woman's head jerks in my direction, but the anxiety in her expression vanishes when our eyes meet. I may secretly be a monster, but good looks, charm, and an expensive haircut ensure I'm not the sort who frightens women when I show up behind them on the street.

"Hi," she says. "Are you here for the wake?"

I shake my head. "No, but I'm a friend of the family." I hold out my hand. "Gabe."

"Aoife," she says, one hand fluttering to her chest before she takes mine and gives it a quick squeeze. "I'm the kids' oldest sister."

I nod, concealing my surprise. So this is the older sister who ran off with her drug-dealer boyfriend, leaving her two-month-old baby behind. This is the woman whose disregard for her responsibilities forced Caitlin to drop out of school, lose her scholarship to an exclusive college preparatory program, and take over raising her niece and three little brothers when she was only seventeen years old.

And now Aoife is back, pregnant again, and wearing a wedding ring…

Getting to the bottom of the prodigal big sister's sudden return would have been enough to convince me to stick around for a few more minutes, even if, at that moment, a van hadn't pulled into the Cooney driveway and slammed on its brakes.

Aoife and I both turn toward the new arrival as the driver's door slams with a sharp *whump*, and a redhead, with wild curls and wilder eyes, rushes around the front of the vehicle. She makes it halfway across the patchy grass of the front yard before she staggers to a stop, her jaw dropping as she shakes her head slowly back and forth.

The girl looks familiar, and I'm about to say hello, when she shouts—

"Holy fucking shit!"

Aoife jumps, startled, and I take a step in front of her, not sure what's wrong, but certain it must have something to do with me, since this woman can't pull her eyes away from my face. I'm assuming we must have a past—maybe I had a thing for redheads before Caitlin and I got together—when the woman lets out a hysterical burst of laughter.

"You're alive," she shouts, pulling in a breath that emerges as a sob. "You're fucking alive. Jesus Christ. Jesus fucking Christ."

The van's side door slides open, and a sleepy voice from inside asks, "What's wrong, Sherry?"

I hear that voice, and my heart stops.

Time slows to a crawl.

It feels like it takes hours to turn my head, an eternity for my gaze to shift from the redhead's face to the face of the woman emerging from the van. And then I meet *her* eyes—pale green eyes above a freckled nose and full lips I've dreamed about kissing too many times to count—and I forget how to breathe.

It's *her*, standing on the cracked driveway in wrinkled khaki shorts and a pale, yellow tee shirt. It's Caitlin. She's here. She's here and real and beautiful and *alive*. So alive, I can smell her smoke and spice scent drifting across the yard, and swear I hear her pulse race as she meets my gaze and a hundred emotions fly across her face.

Shock is followed closely by confusion, pain, and then a look of joy so naked it feels like an invasion of privacy to watch it light up her features. I should look away, but I can't. I'm afraid to look away, afraid to blink, for fear that by the time I open my eyes, she will have vanished all over again.

"Gabe?" The word bleeds hope, her voice so raw it's painful to hear.

Yes, I want to say. *Thank God you're okay.* But I can't seem to force my lips to move.

"Gabe?" she repeats before I can recover the ability to speak. "Please, say something."

"Yes," I say, voice breaking in the middle of the word.

I know I should say more. I should tell her everything I've thought and felt and feared for the past year, but I don't know how to start. I should go to her, pull her into my arms, and show her how fucking relieved I am to see her, but I can't seem to take a step forward. All I can do is stand at the edge of the street, staring, feeling like my heart is splitting open and Caitlin is rushing in to banish the emptiness that's been with me since the surgery.

Only now, looking into her eyes, do I realize that the hole inside of me is in the exact shape of this girl, and that—even more than my lost memories—it is the loss of *her* that has made me feel so incomplete.

"It's really you," she whispers after a long, silent moment, shaking her head back and forth like she still can't believe it. "Oh my God. Oh…my God."

Her hands fly up to cover her mouth as she bursts into tears. She cries like a dam breaking, like a tidal wave rushing toward the shore. Her tears are terrifying, and some part of me realizes they're dangerous, even before she starts gasping for breath.

"Caitlin, are you okay?" The redhead starts toward Caitlin, but before she takes two steps, Caitlin's eyes roll back and her knees buckle. She hits the ground with a muffled thud that is apparently what I needed to jolt my body into action.

I lunge forward, jumping onto the sidewalk and sprinting across the grass. I kneel next to Caitlin and gather her limp body into my arms, heart slamming against my ribs as a dark voice inside my head insists I've killed her.

I know it's not true; I know she's only fainted. I know it the way I know that fairy tales don't come true, and a kiss never brought a beautiful girl back from the dead. But still, I'm terrified that I've lost her all over again, and the only thing I can think to do is kiss her, so I cradle the back of her head in my palm, and press my lips to hers.

For a long moment, there is nothing but softness, and the faint pressure of her teeth, firm against my lips, but then her breath rushes out. Her eyelashes flutter against my cheek, and her arms twine around my neck. She pulls me close with a strength that's surprising, and kisses me with enough passion to light a city through an endless winter.

She kisses me, and *I* am the one brought back to life.

The moment her tongue slips between my lips, I remember the way it was with us, the way she made me feel so fucking alive, vibrating at a frequency so high and sweet it can only be heard by magical creatures and people who are purely, desperately, endlessly in love.

At that moment, sitting in the dust and brown grass, with her warm in my arms, I make a vow that I will have it all again.

I will have Caitlin and magic and the life we

dreamed of together, back before something ripped us apart.

CHAPTER

Caitlin

*"You're something between a
dream and a miracle."*
-Elizabeth Barrett Browning

*I*t's not real. People don't come back from the
dead. This is just another horrible dream. It
isn't real.
This. Isn't. Real.

My head spills out an endless, silent litany
of despair, but my heart is shattering with
happiness. Every cell in my body is catching
fire, shining so bright I could illuminate a
universe, because Gabe is alive.

He is *alive* and I'm never, *ever* going to let
him go.

I pull him closer and he presses his lips harder to mine, kissing me with the hunger I've missed so much. Our tongues tangle and his taste floods my senses and it is the best taste, the sweetest, most miraculous taste. It breaks my heart only to heal it and break it all over again, but I don't care. I don't care that this moment is so beautiful that it hurts. I don't care about anything except the fact that Gabe is in my arms.

We hold each other so close my ribs feel like they're bruising, but it still isn't close enough. I need to be closer, I need to thread my spirit through his bones so tight no one will ever be able to tear us apart again.

"You're here," I whisper against his lips. "You're really here."

"I tried to find you, but I couldn't," he says, his fingers digging into my skull, that hint of discomfort enough to confirm that this isn't a dream.

Gabe is alive. *Alive.*

"She told me you were dead," I sob, clutching at his shoulders when he tries to pull away, refusing to let his body move more than a few inches from mine.

"What?"

"Your mother. She told me you were dead," I repeat, the words coming faster. "I didn't want to believe her. You hadn't been admitted to any hospital, and none of the funeral homes had your body. So I broke into Darby Hill, looking for clues, but I found an email, and ashes, and then your father sent me a letter telling me I shouldn't come to the funeral." I pull in a shuddery breath, but I refuse to start crying again.

"I don't understand." Gabe's brows pull together. "Whose funeral?"

"Yours. They had a funeral. For you," I say, knowing I'm rambling, but too keyed up to stop. "Or they faked a funeral to make sure I stopped looking for you. I don't know. I have no idea how they could do this, how they could—"

"Hold on a second." Gabe blinks and uncertainty flickers in his ice blue eyes, those eyes I've dreamed about so many times, but have been positive I would never look into again. "You think my parents faked my death?"

"They did," Sherry pipes up, reminding me that we have an audience. "I know it sounds crazy, but I was there. I saw the letter your dad sent."

I glance up to see Sherry standing behind Gabe with the kids gathered around her. Sean and Ray looked stunned, Emmie still seems sleepy from the nap we took in the van on the way here from the airport, but it is Danny's expression that catches my attention. Danny is staring down at me with an "oh shit" look on his face I haven't seen since the time I caught him drinking one of Dad's beers when he was eleven years old, and lit into him with enough fire and brimstone to make sure he hasn't looked sideways at an alcoholic beverage since.

I can't imagine what has him so spooked, but then his eyes shift to his left and my gaze follows, and there she is—my big sister, Aoife. She's wearing a gauzy floral sundress, and practically glowing with health. She looks more like a kindergarten teacher than the strung out mess I remember, a transformation that, with Gabe back from the grave, is too much for my brain to make sense of.

Our eyes meet, and a nervous smile flickers at the edges of her lips.

"Hey," she says. "Should I come back later? This seems like…a weird time."

My first instinct is to tell her to go and never come back—we've managed for four years without her, and I have bigger things to deal with—but then I realize she must be here for the wake. No matter what a shit mother and big sister she's been, I can't very well tell her she's not allowed to mourn her father.

"Can you give me a couple of hours?" I ask in a tight voice as Gabe helps me to my feet and stands beside me. For a moment, I feel the loss of his touch like a physical blow, weakening my knees, but then he takes my hand and my knees firm up again. I look up at him, holding his gaze as I tell Aoife, "There's a lot going on right now."

"I understand," she says, then adds in an upbeat tone. "Would it help if I took the kids with me? We could catch up, give you two some privacy. Maybe I could take everyone for ice cream, if we can find a place that's open this early?"

I open my mouth to say "hell no," but Sean is already shouting that he wants two scoops of mint chocolate chip, and Emmie is smiling up at Aoife, clearly willing to accept this stranger as a friend if she's offering ice cream. Emmie discovered a passion for raspberry sorbet a few months ago. Since then, she has been willing to eat any number of previously reviled vegetables in order to earn her scoop of dessert after I'm finished cleaning up dinner.

She, of course, has no idea that the woman offering to buy her a treat is the mother who abandoned her. The mother who never called, sent a single email, or offered so much as a dime to help cover the costs of raising a child. The mother who has no idea that her daughter has struggled to meet so many developmental milestones because she was using drugs and drinking for four months before she realized she was pregnant. For years, I've wanted to tell my sister all of it, to tell her how deeply she fucked up, and watch her face crumple as she realizes what a waste she is.

Now, I just want her to disappear. I don't have time for Aoife, or anger, or anything else, but Gabe.

"I'll go with them," Sherry says, obviously sensing that I don't want Aoife left alone with the kids. "You two take all the time you need."

I nod, silently thanking her, my heart flipping in my chest when she smiles and tears rush down her cheeks. She knows how monumental this is, and I know she's as happy for me as if it were the love of her life who had just been resurrected.

"Okay, guys. Let's get buckled up." Sherry herds the kids toward the van before turning back to Aoife with raised eyebrows. "You want to meet us at Two Scoops?"

"Sounds perfect. Meet you there," Aoife

says, starting toward a silver car parked at the curb. It's only when she turns that I notice the telltale roundness beneath her dress.

I realize she's pregnant, and my breath rushes out like I've been punched. The pain of losing Gabe's and my baby hits all over again, made fresh by the realization that I'll have to tell him what happened. I'll have to tell Gabe that I lost our child, that he was a boy, and that I loved him so much it hurt, even though he was dead before he left my body. I have so many things to tell the man I love, so many awful things, but the awful things are now suddenly bearable because he is alive.

Alive.

The word keeps exploding in my brain, destroying everything I thought I knew was true. But it is the best kind of devastation. It's a flood wiping the earth clean, giving me a chance at the life I was so certain I'd lost.

I turn back to Gabe as Sherry pulls the van out of the driveway, staring up into his face, memorizing the slope of his cheekbones and the way his dark lashes flare around his eyes and his hair falls over his forehead. I don't ever want to look away. I want to stand here staring until this feels real, until I know he isn't going to disappear the moment I turn my back.

"I don't know where to start," I say, breath rushing out.

"It's all right." He brushes my tangled hair behind my ear, reminding me I must look a mess after the long flight and my nap in the van. But it doesn't matter. The way Gabe's looking at me leaves no doubt I'm the most beautiful thing he's seen in ages.

"We'll figure everything out," he continues. "I'm just so glad you're okay. I recovered a memory of you a couple of weeks ago that…scared me."

My forehead wrinkles. "Recovered?"

"I had the surgery." Gabe turns his head, lifting his thick, nearly black, hair with one hand, revealing a long, pink scar. "Since then my memories have been patchy."

"Oh my God," I say softly, letting my fingers brush across the puckered skin. "But you're okay? You're better?"

"I'm tumor free." He drops his hand, letting his hair fall into place as he turns back to me. "But I lost most of last summer. The memories have been coming back, but it's slow. I didn't remember your name until January, and it's only been in the past few months that I've remembered…other things."

"Other things," I repeat numbly, my pulse

thudding unhealthily in my temple. Gabe lost most of last summer.

Lost. That means he lost the months we fell in love, and all the memories of who we were together.

I'm already starting to panic even before Gabe says—

"I know we used to steal things, but I don't remember why." He glances over his shoulder toward the house before continuing in a softer voice. "And then, a few weeks ago, I had this memory of my hands at someone's throat, and an image of you, your neck covered in bruises. After that, I was afraid."

"Afraid of what?" The thud in my temples becomes a pain that digs into the back of my eyes. Surely he can't mean...

"I was afraid I had...hurt you," Gabe says, looking down at me with shame in his blue eyes.

Shame.

Gabe doesn't do shame. He rarely does regret. I've heard Gabe say he was sorry a handful of times, but I've only seen him genuinely filled with regret once. It was the night we killed Pitt, but he didn't regret the murder. He regretted the lies he'd told, and that he'd let us fall so deep in love when he knew he would be dead before the year was out.

And now he's standing in front of me, alive, but missing pieces of what made him the man he was. The old Gabe would never have thought that he was capable of hurting me, not for a second. The old Gabe would have fought for me, killed for me, died for me. I knew it, and he knew it. It was the kind of thing that went unspoken between us, so obvious that there was no need to say the words.

Sure, the old Gabe wasn't your conventional, upstanding citizen, but he was a man who knew himself, inside and out, and made choices based on his own marrow-deep beliefs in what was right and wrong. They weren't the same things society calls right and wrong, but Gabe's convictions were stronger because he had worked through the big questions and come up with his own, authentic answers. But now, he seems to have lost touch with those answers, and may have lost more than just his memories of last summer.

What if he's lost the parts of him that made him unlike anyone I've ever met, the parts he was so afraid of losing, he chose to die rather than risk a surgery that might leave him profoundly changed?

The thought is so awful that, for a moment, it feels like Gabe has died all over again, only worse. Now, he is alive, but with a mind that believes he's capable of hurting someone he loves, and a heart that could never love me the way I love him. Even if he recovers his memories, the man who made them might never return.

I take a step back, tears blurring my vision. I'm turning to run—somewhere, anywhere—when Gabe's fingers wrap around my upper arms, holding me in place with that same tender strength I remember.

"Don't go," he says, voice hoarse and as pained as I feel. "I know this is hard, but you have to know how badly I want to remember. I want to remember everything about you, about *us*, but I don't yet, no matter how hard I've tried."

He pauses, tongue slipping out to dampen his lips, making me think of our kiss, and how it had felt like our old kisses. "But I remember that I loved you, and that you were the only person who ever made me feel worth a damn. And when I kissed you just now...I felt alive for the first time since I woke up with part of my brain gone and this feeling that something vital was missing." He pins me with that look that always made me feel like he knew all my

27

secrets. "That vital thing is *you*."

"How can it be me?" I ask, tears filling my eyes. "You don't even know me."

"I know you," he insists, with an intensity more consistent with the Gabe I knew at the end of last summer than the arrogant boy I first met. "If I were blind, I would know you. You're the reason I've kept going, even when recovery threatened to kick my ass, and all I wanted to do was give up. I might have lost our past, Caitlin, but we don't have to lose our future. We can get *us* back. I know we can."

I stare deep into his eyes, seeing hope and that familiar Gabe passion, but something is missing, something I can't ignore now that I've realized it's not there.

"But you don't love me," I whisper, knowing I'll start sobbing again if I say the words too loud.

"But I did," he says, his grip loosening, becoming a caress as his fingers skim down my arms to capture my hands. "I remember I did."

I pull my hands away. "Remembering you used to love someone, and loving them, isn't the same thing."

"Then I'll just have to fall in love all over again," he says, his words almost a perfect echo of what I said last summer.

As soon as I found out about the tumor, I'd begged Gabe to have the surgery, insisting that I would make him fall in love with me a second time if he came out on the other side not remembering who I was. But now I'm faced with the reality of a Gabe who doesn't remember why we robbed people, or the rush we felt when we were dispensing our own brand of justice. This Gabe doesn't remember the murder we committed, or the reasons he believed we had no choice but to kill the man who kidnapped me.

He doesn't remember the way he made love to me that last night, fucking me until we were both bruised with pleasure, while promising to love me until men were fairy tales. He doesn't remember the secrets we shared, or that he was my first, or that he saw the strength in me when no else did, or a hundred other things that are the reasons there will never be anyone in my heart but Gabe Alexander.

I don't know how to start over with a new Gabe, when I'm still in love with the boy I knew before, but I have to try. This thing with him has never been easy, but it is the only thing worth having.

I knew that two days ago, when I broke up with Isaac before the kids and I got ready to fly to South Carolina. I told him we were going to the Big Island for a vacation with Sherry, and that he should take the ten days we were gone to move out. I knew if he learned that Chuck had died, he'd insist on coming to the funeral and I didn't want Isaac stress on top of burying-my-father stress. And once I'd decided to break up, I couldn't put it off. I'd finally admitted that friendship and sweet lovemaking were never going to be enough for me, and I didn't want to settle for less for even a few more days.

I wanted passion and fire, I wanted to walk up to the edge of oblivion and stare into the chaos on the other side. I wanted Gabe, and now, miraculously, I have another shot with the man I thought I'd lost forever. I would be a weak, pathetic, coward to shy away from that, simply because our second chance is going to be difficult.

My entire life has been difficult. If I'm equipped for anything, it's digging my heels in and getting through the hard shit.

"You're going to say yes," Gabe says, his lips twisting to one side the way they do when he's getting what he wants. "I can tell. I remember this face."

I take a breath, and a tiny flame of hope flickers back to life inside me. "What else do you remember? I want to know everything."

"Me too," he says. "You want to get out of here? Go someplace private where we can be alone to talk?"

I meet his eyes and I can tell he isn't thinking about talking, but no matter how much I'd love to let Gabe whisk me away to his father's abandoned office, or the barn in his parents' back forty, or some lonely gravel road so far from civilization no one would hear me scream his name, I don't want sex to come first. Our sexual connection was amazing, but I don't want to make love to Gabe again until I know we're both emotionally invested. Making love to him, while he simply fucked me, would break my heart.

"We can go into the backyard," I say. "This is Veronica's house now, so I wouldn't feel right going inside without knocking, and I think it's best to let her sleep as long as possible. She left a couple of messages on my phone last night while we were in the air. Sounded like she'd had a few."

"Is she going to notice we're walking around outside?"

"I doubt it," I say, leading the way across the grass. "And even if she does, she'll be cool. She's actually a pretty decent person."

"Better than Chuck deserved?" Gabe asks in a wry tone.

I swallow past the lump in my throat. "Maybe. I don't know. My dad was better near the end. I sort of wish I'd made more of an effort with him."

Gabe stops walking several feet from the picnic table under the shade tree. I turn, not liking the look on his face. "What?"

His brows draw together, reminding me that Gabe is beautiful, even when he's frowning. "I don't know if I should tell you on the day of your father's wake."

"Tell me," I say. "If it's about Chuck, not much could surprise me."

Gabe studies me for a moment before he nods, evidently deciding to take me at my word. "I came here looking for you last January. Chuck answered the door."

My features flinch, as if they can't figure out what kind of face to make in response to the bomb Gabe's just dropped. "Wh-what? Are you sure it was him?"

"I'm sure. I asked if he knew where you were, but he said you'd run off, and he hadn't seen you since last summer. He said you'd left the kids alone, and he'd sent them to live with his sister in Florida not long after."

Pain flashes through my chest as I struggle

to wrap my head around this latest betrayal. How could Chuck do this? How could he keep something like *Gabe being alive* from me? How could even *he* be such a complete and utter bastard?

"I was wrong," I say, fighting to breathe past the painful knot fisting in my chest. "I guess Chuck still has a few surprises left in him, after all."

"Maybe he thought he was doing you a favor?" Gabe asks, pity in his eyes. "I remember he wasn't a fan of you and me."

I shake my head. "No, he knew how much I loved you, and how devastated I was when you died." I shake my head again, a little harder. "When I *thought* you'd died."

"I'm so sorry. No one should have to go through what you've been through." Gabe steps closer, pulling me against him. I go willingly, wrapping my arms around his waist and pressing my face to his white polo shirt, inhaling the miraculous scent of him.

"Even thinking I might have lost you..." He takes in a breath and lets it out long and slow. "It was unthinkable. Especially knowing I might have been the one responsible."

I lift my head, tilting my chin up until I can see his face. "But you had to know you would never hurt me. *Never.* I can't even imagine it."

He meets my gaze and the relief in his eyes is palpable. "I didn't want to believe I would, but my parents said the tumor changed me. And I don't remember why we did the things we did, the robberies and…all the rest of it. Especially the rest of it."

I can tell by his tone he means the murder. "A man named Ned Pitt kidnapped me," I begin softly, filling Gabe in on the events of the night Pitt lost his life and we burned his house to the ground. By the time I'm finished, Gabe doesn't look relieved. He looks furious, merciless, the way he did when he was standing next to the mattress where we'd dumped Pitt's body, preparing to set it on fire.

"That explains how angry I am in those memories," Gabe says. "All I can think about is how much I want to kill whoever I've got my hands on. I swear I can taste blood in my mouth, but I can't get a clear picture of the person's face."

"You were in a lot of pain," I say. "You were blacking out. That's how I found out about the tumor."

Gabe's eyes open wider and his lips tighten. He doesn't say a word, but I can still read him as well as I could before.

"You didn't remember that you didn't tell me." I don't wait for Gabe to confirm my suspicion. "It's okay. I wasn't angry. I understood."

He's quiet for a moment before he says, "How could you?"

"Neither of us planned on falling in love," I say with a shrug. "We made a promise to each other that we wouldn't. We were only supposed to be together for the summer. Just one wild summer."

"But we fell in love anyway," Gabe says, meeting my eyes with a hopeful look. "Should be easy to fall in love again if we're actually trying."

As long as ghosts don't get in our way, I think. Aloud I say—

"You want to come to the wake with me? I would rather not let you out of my sight, if that's okay with you."

He nods. "That's perfect. Should I go home and change?"

I shake my head. "Shorts and tee shirts are fine. The Cooneys don't stand on ceremony. Besides, I think it's better if we keep us a secret, at least until we figure out why your parents lied."

"And your dad, too," Gabe reminds me, eyes narrowing as he glances toward the house. "You don't think they were in on it together, do you?"

I frown. "I don't see how. I doubt Chuck ever met your parents. They didn't exactly run in the same social circles."

"No, they didn't." Gabe nods, but I can tell he isn't ready to let this go. "Still, we shouldn't rule it out. We should start a file and keep all the information we collect together. Sooner or later, we'll figure out what happened, and who's responsible."

"And then what?" I ask, excitement making my belly flutter. He sounds like the old Gabe, when we were putting together a plan for a new job.

"Then we make it clear to my parents, and anyone else involved, that they aren't allowed to interfere in our lives ever again," he says, a dangerous note in his voice that makes my heart join in the fluttering.

Maybe the old Gabe and the new Gabe aren't so different, after all.

CHAPTER
Four

Gabe

*"When beggars die, there are no comets seen;
The heavens themselves blaze forth the death of
princes."*-Shakespeare

The day passes with infinite slowness.

I call my mother and apologize for missing our lunch date. I tell her I'm too tired from my ride to get cleaned up, ignore her obvious irritation, and settle into my first Irish-Catholic wake.

It involves a lot more drinking than any funeral-type event I've been to before, but it's not a bad scene. Aside from the body in the back room that Caitlin views for only a few moments before carefully keeping the rest of the kids away from their embalmed father, it's a fairly festive event.

Chuck's girlfriend is welcoming, and I'm happy to see the kids—especially Emmie, who gives me a hug as soon as she walks in the door, though I can't believe she remembers me—but tipping my glass to a man who lied to keep me and Caitlin apart isn't the way I want to spend my first day back with the woman I've been dreaming about every night for the past six months. I want to be alone with her. I want to kiss every inch of her body, and make her come calling my name. I want to hold her close afterward, and whisper whatever it takes to banish the doubt and fear in her eyes. I'm different than I was, and it's obvious she sees that, but I know I can be the man she loved again.

Every doctor I've met with since the surgery has said the same thing—even if the memories are intact, it will take time for the brain to form new neural pathways to access old information—but right now I feel like I could slash my way through the overgrown jungle of my mind in a single night, if I could just get Caitlin alone…

But we are surrounded by Chuck's girlfriend's friends, a dozen of Chuck's drinking buddies from the local dive, who have come for the free beer, and a shifting stream of people from the neighborhood, dropping by out of respect for the family. Caitlin is kept busy greeting visitors and helping Veronica hand out beer and snacks, but even in her few moments of downtime, there's not much of a chance for us to talk. Caitlin holds my hand, or threads her arm through mine, but her attention has been captured by her sister, newly returned from God knows where.

Aoife holds court at the kitchen table, laughing with old friends excited to see her back in town, while she helps Emmie make rubber band friendship bracelets with a kit Caitlin brought to keep the kids entertained. The nearly four-year-old's slender arm is already half covered with bracelets, but she can't seem to get enough. She stays on Aoife's lap for almost an hour, during which I'm pretty sure Caitlin is going to grind her teeth to nubs.

"Relax," I whisper. "She's a novelty. The thrill will wear off."

"Aoife's up to something," Caitlin whispers back. "I don't know what, but she wouldn't come back just for Chuck's funeral. She hated him."

"So did you," I remind her.

She sighs as she turns away from the cozy scene to stare out the curtains into the front yard, where the boys are playing horseshoes with a few of Chuck's friends from the bar. "I just wish I knew why he lied."

"I'd like to know that, too. I'll search my mother's and father's home offices tonight. See if I can find a Chuck connection, or make sense of the ashes you found."

"They were a prop," Caitlin says bitterly. "Part of the lie."

I make a considering sound. Caitlin's mind is made up, but I don't understand why my parents would go to such drastic lengths. It's not as if they knew Caitlin was going to break into Darby Hill. Caitlin assured me no one but Ned Pitt knew about our illegal activities, and we made sure he didn't have the chance to share the news with anyone.

I don't know how to feel about the fact that Caitlin and I killed a man together. Or, more accurately, I don't know how to feel about the fact that I'm glad the man is dead. Learning the truth put my mind at ease for the first time in weeks. I didn't murder an innocent; I helped take out an abomination who would have been spending his life in jail if my father didn't excel at defending criminals.

I'm supposed to go back to school in the fall to finish my pre-law degree, then head to law school, and eventually end up back in Giffney, where I'll join the practice my father and grandfather built. It's all planned out, my entire life stretching out before me like a freshly paved road. But now I'm starting to see the cracks in the shiny surface and the tempting places to turn off that would allow me to head in a completely different direction.

"Caitlin, can I put on my swimsuit?" comes a high, sweet voice from near the couch.

Caitlin and I turn from the window to find Emmie bouncing up and down on her bare feet, a giddy expression on her face. "Mama says she'll put up the Slip 'N Slide in the back yard. Can I have my suit on now?"

I glance sideways, not surprised to see Caitlin's face draining of color and her lips pressing into a thin, angry line. When Aoife rises from her chair at the dining table and crosses the room, I half expect Caitlin to lift her small fists and start swinging.

Instead, she smiles and lifts a brow. "Mama?"

"She was having a hard time saying my name," Aoife explains, resting her hands on Emmie's thin shoulders. "I thought 'mama' would be easier."

"It's Ee Fuh, Emmie," Caitlin says, her gaze not leaving Aoife's face. "Ee, like in street, and Fuh like Fuh-ged-about-it." She does the last part in an accent that makes Emmie laugh.

"Fuh-ged-about-it," Emmie repeats, giggling again. "Ee Fuh-ged-about-it."

"Perfect!" Caitlin bends down, grinning as she tickles Emmie's ribs.

Emmie laughs hard enough to send her shoulders sliding out from under her mother's hands. The moment she's free, Caitlin swoops Emmie into her arms and kisses her flushed cheek.

"And I have a better idea than the Slip 'N Slide." Caitlin rests her forehead on Emmie's. "How about we go check into our hotel and try out the pool? You and Sean can show Gabe what good swimmers you are now."

Emmie's eyes light up. "Pool! Yay, pool!"

"Get your sandals on, and go let the boys know," Caitlin says, setting Emmie back on her feet. "Tell them we're leaving in five minutes."

Aoife looks less than pleased with the sudden departure, but she doesn't say a word until Emmie is out of earshot, the front door slamming closed behind her.

"I'm her mother, Caitlin," Aoife says. "There's nothing wrong with her calling me mama if she wants to."

"I'm not going to have this conversation right now," Caitlin says in a voice like ice. "In fact, I'm *never* going to have this conversation. As soon as the funeral is over tomorrow, I want you gone."

Aoife sighs, but the look in her eyes is anything but defeated. "I didn't want to discuss this until after we finished everything for Dad, but…there's another reason I'm here."

"Of course there is." Caitlin's smile is viciously sweet. "I wouldn't expect anything else, but I don't know what you're hoping to get. Chuck left Veronica this house, and he signed Aunt Sarah's place over to me last summer. There may still be some of Aunt Sarah's money left in his account, but you and Veronica will have to fight it out for that."

"I didn't come here for money," Aoife snaps. "I came for my daughter. When I go back to Florida in a week, I want Emmie to come with me."

Caitlin's eyes widen slightly, but when she speaks she sounds amused. "Emmie is staying with me, and the boys—the people who love her, and have always been there for her. You're out of your mind if you think I'm letting a stranger take her away."

"I'm not a stranger, I'm her mother."

Aoife's voice rises, attracting the attention of the older women drinking in the kitchen, who stop laughing and turn to peer into the living room. "And it's not your decision to make. I appreciate everything you've done, but—"

"But nothing," Caitlin says, still calm and collected. "You lost your chance to play the mother card when you left your daughter hungry and crying in her crib, and didn't call, write, or send a dime for four years."

"So you want money?" Aoife asks. "If that's it, I've got it. I'm married now, and Mitch has a good job. We've got a house with a pool in a beautiful gated community. We can give Emmie everything, even a baby sister in four months."

Aoife caresses her stomach with one hand, and I feel Caitlin stiffen beside me. "She'll be happy with us," Aoife continues with a dreamy smile, as if she's already watching Emmie's perfect new life play out behind her eyes. "Mitch understands that I was young and messed up when I left my daughter. But he's forgiven me, and he wants me to bring Emmie home. He's going to adopt her, and we'll be a family."

"Mitch sounds like a swell guy," Caitlin says, sarcasm dripping from the words. "But the court awarded me full guardianship of

Emmie last summer. I'm her legal caregiver. She's flying back to Hawaii with me when I leave in ten days, and that's the end of the discussion."

Aoife's nostrils flare, but when she speaks again, her voice is as cool as Caitlin's. "You don't get to decide that."

"I sure as hell do," Caitlin says, her hands balling into fists at her sides, making me worry that the brawl I thought I saw coming a few minutes ago might be happening after all. "In every way that counts, *I'm* Emmie's mother. You're just an egg donor."

The women eavesdropping across the room suck in a scandalized breath, and Aoife lifts her chin. "You can say whatever you want to hurt me, but I *am* Emmie's mother, and I have rights. I was hoping we could keep things from getting nasty, but if you're not willing to do what's best for my daughter, we can take this to court."

"You don't give a shit about what's best for Emmie. This is about you, the way everything always is." Caitlin steps closer, before adding in a whisper, "But you will *never* take that little girl away from her family. Do you hear me? I will destroy you first."

The words are so soft I know no one but Aoife and I heard them, but they still lift the hairs on the back of my neck. Caitlin isn't making idle threats. When it comes to defending her family, she doesn't fuck around.

The thought is followed by a flash of memory. I see Caitlin straddling a man—Pitt, on the night he chained Caitlin up in his attic. She's half naked, with tears running down her face, but I can see the determination in the way her muscles strain and her hands lock around his neck. I watch the agony creasing her features become resolve and then a strangely peaceful expression that is chilling, even on a girl barely five feet tall. She steps over the threshold from prey to predator without a single look over her shoulder. I remember thinking at the time that she was like a dark angel, beautiful and deadly.

But what do I think now?

I don't know, only that I doubt Aoife understands how dangerous it can be to get on Caitlin's bad side.

I'm still half lost in the memory when Caitlin takes my hand and starts toward the door. I thread my fingers through hers and follow her out into the hot, humid day, but for the first time since I pulled her back into my arms, I wonder what I've gotten myself into. Once upon a time, I was the kind of man who could not only handle Caitlin's dark side, but match it, shadow for shadow. We were a perfect pair, but now…

I don't know if I can be the person I was, and I'm not sure I want to be. The straight and narrow path my parents have laid out for me doesn't feel right, but careening down a winding road at a hundred miles per hour, flattening anyone who gets in my way, doesn't, either.

"Okay guys, load up," Caitlin shouts to the kids before lifting her hand to Sherry. Her friend stands near the road next to two men smoking cigarettes. The guys look about our age—wearing the same faded jeans and tee shirts from high school, but with the start of the beer bellies that come to early twenty-somethings who drink a six pack every night—but I don't remember meeting them before.

Though that doesn't mean much lately…

"Sherry, I'm going to head to the hotel and let the kids swim," Caitlin says. "You want to come with us, or do you want to catch a ride over later?"

"I'll catch a ride over," Sherry says, smiling when she sees we're holding hands, blissfully ignorant to the sisterly showdown that took place inside the house, or all the conflicted thoughts racing through my mind. "Have fun!"

"Doubtful," Caitlin mutters beneath her breath as she starts for the van. "I'm sorry about this," she adds, glancing over at me. "Aoife always did have shit timing."

"It's all right," I say. "Too bad you and my dad are on the outs, or I could probably get him to represent you for free."

Caitlin freezes a few feet from the van, where Danny is helping Emmie get buckled into her booster seat and Ray and Sean are arguing about whose turn it is to sit in the back.

"We're not on the *outs*, Gabe," Caitlin says, frowning up at me. "He wrote me a letter telling me not to come to your funeral. He and your mom *faked your death* to keep us apart, and I, for one, would like to see them rot in hell for it. You need to believe me about this, okay?"

"I believe you," I say, though a part of me is still hoping there has been some insane mix up that will allow Caitlin to be confused, and my parents to be redeemed.

They've lied about how much they knew about my relationship with Caitlin, but I assumed it was because she wasn't the sort of girl they wanted me tangled up with. I know in my parents' eyes—my mother's, especially—a girl without a pedigree, and good standing at an Ivy League school, is beneath me. Deborah would see a girl like Caitlin as a weight that would drag me down, and Mom wouldn't be above pretending not to remember her in the name of sending me back to college a free agent.

"Are you sure?" Caitlin asks, hurt in her eyes. "Because you don't look like you believe me. You look like you think I'm crazy."

"I don't think you're crazy." I reach out, but she takes a step back before I can touch her, making it clear this isn't something I'm going to be able to sweep under the rug.

"I promise, I don't think you're crazy," I say in my most soothing tone. "But I *am* hoping there is some other explanation."

"Like what?" Caitlin asks, shaking her head.

I lift my hands. "I don't know. Just give me a chance to have a look around Darby Hill and see what I can find. I've looked through my parents' emails before, but maybe I didn't go back far enough, or—"

"You do that." Caitlin cuts me off in the same cool tone she used with Aoife. "And if you can't find anything, and decide to believe your parents have your best interests at heart, then…good for you. But I will promise you this…"

49

She glances toward the van where the kids are obviously trying to eavesdrop—they've left the van door open and are being quieter than they've been all day. She steps closer and lowers her voice. "The Gabe I used to know understood that his parents were horrible, and he did everything he could to be the opposite of the selfish, heartless people who raised him."

"The Gabe you knew was also dying," I say, frustration creeping into my tone. "I'm not."

She's quiet for a moment, but the steel in her eyes doesn't waver. "Yes, the Gabe I knew was dying. But he trusted me with all the life he had left, and he would never have doubted my word. Not for a second."

She turns and moves around the front of the van, moving so quickly I have to jog to, catch the door in my hand before she slams it. "So that's it? You're just going to run away?"

"I'm not running away. I'm taking the kids swimming."

"Don't play games," I say, anger making my fingers press harder into the metal of the door. "I don't know everything, but I know that's not the way we were together."

Her calm mask falters, but she doesn't move to get out of the van. "Well...maybe we have further to go to get back to the way we were than we thought."

"Maybe we do." I brace my other hand on the warm aluminum of the window frame. "And maybe you're going to have to meet me halfway."

She lifts one pale brow. "Meaning?"

"I'm not on board for anything like what you told me about this morning," I say carefully, aware the kids are listening. "I want to keep things on the level from here on out."

Caitlin's jaw drops and for a second I think I've rendered her speechless, but then she says, "You are a piece of work, Gabe Alexander. Only *you* could make me want to slap you the same day I think I'm going to die from happiness that you're alive."

She hauls on the door, and I let it go, wincing as she slams the door hard enough to shake the entire van. Before I can step away from the door, she shifts the vehicle into reverse and peels down the driveway into the street.

I stand, watching her leave with a nasty sinking feeling in my chest.

I clearly don't know how to handle Caitlin Cooney anymore, but I sure as fuck don't like watching her drive away.

CHAPTER
Five

Caitlin

"Alas, I have grieved so I am hard to love.
Yet love—wilt thou?"
-Elizabeth Barrett Browning

By the time I get the younger kids into their swimsuits and down to the hotel pool, regret is swelling inside my stomach, making me feel like I've swallowed a balloon filled with poison.

He's alive; that's all that matters. He's alive, and he wants to love me again. It's every impossible dream come true, and I turned my back on it and drove away. I shouldn't have left the way I did, no matter how much it hurt to listen to him defend the people who made the past year the most miserable of my life—and from a person raised by my mother and father, that's saying something.

But Gabe's been through hell, too, and lost pieces of himself through no fault of his own. He clearly doesn't remember all the reasons why he used to loathe his parents. I, on the other hand, remember everything, and I owe it to Gabe to help him to the truth, to hold his hand as he pulls back the curtains and discovers all the dirty secrets Aaron and Deborah are hiding.

I call him from a deck chair by the pool, intending to apologize and ask him to come join us at the hotel, but I get a message that the number is no longer in service.

I hang up with a frustrated sigh. I should have known Aaron and Deborah wouldn't let Gabe keep his old number. They wanted him to have a fresh start so badly they faked his death. Getting him a new cell phone number is nothing compared to the ashes, or the funeral invitation, or the official letter from their lawyer announcing that they were contesting Gabe's will, and I wouldn't be receiving the trust fund money he'd wanted to leave me anytime soon.

"You're sure there's nothing?" I ask Sherry when she calls from the hotel room, having graciously offered to do some recon online while I watch over the kids at the pool.

"I've looked through all the newspaper archives," she says. "There was never any mention of Gabe's funeral, or a memorial service, or anything. Not even in the society page, which is totally fishy since they like to document it every time the Alexanders take an interesting-shaped shit."

I almost smile, but I can't. "I can't believe I didn't notice last summer. I should have realized there was nothing official."

"You got an invitation in the mail, that's pretty official," Sherry says. "Don't you dare beat yourself up about this. There was no reason to think anything was going on except that the Alexanders wanted to keep their son's funeral as private as possible. And that's not that weird, considering he died so young. I mean…" She makes a frustrated, confused sound that I can empathize with. "*Didn't* die. Jesus…what a crazy day."

"I know." I force a smile as Emmie waves to me from the diving board. "I still can't believe it's real. And I don't know what was up with my dad."

"You think the Alexanders paid him off?" Sherry asks. "Gave him some cash to keep quiet about Gabe being back from the dead?"

I shake my head. "I don't know. Gabe said something similar, but it's hard to imagine the Alexanders and my dad even having a conversation, you know? They might as well have been from different planets."

"I hear you," she says, hesitating a moment before she adds. "I'm just so sorry about all this, Caitlin. I keep thinking how everything would have been different if I'd stayed in Giffney. I know we didn't run in the same circles, but I would have run into Gabe sooner or later. And then I could have called you and—"

"If I'm not allowed to get self-blamey, you certainly aren't allowed to," I say, cutting her off before she can go any further down that road. "And honestly, it would have been hellish to do this much sooner. Gabe said he only remembered my name in January, and even now he only has…pieces of our history. There's so much he doesn't remember."

"But he loves you," Sherry says. "You two are soul mates, Caitlin. That much was clear from the way you made out like the world was ending the second you laid eyes on each other."

My cheeks heat for reasons having nothing to do with the August sun beating down on the Residence Inn pool. "Yeah, I bet Danny would be giving me shit about that if he weren't giving me the silent treatment for fighting with Gabe. He's been in the exercise room this entire time watching Sports Center. He wouldn't even look at me when I asked what he wanted for supper."

"He's as confused as the rest of us," Sherry says. "Give him time. He'll come around. Especially when I bring a pizza feast back to the room."

"That reminds me." I stand, stepping farther from the shallow end, where Emmie and Sean are playing Marco Polo. "Don't get pizza from Isaac's dad's place, okay? I don't want them to know we're back. Isaac still thinks we're on the Big Island on vacation."

Sherry sighs. "I know. He's texted me six times today, begging me to talk to you for him, asking if he can take a few days off from work and come meet us before we do the volcano hike. The poor guy is going to be devastated. He's never going to believe you didn't know Gabe was alive when you broke up with him, no matter how many times I'll swear it's true."

"This is the same 'poor guy' who lied to us both, and said you thought I was headed off the deep end," I remind her, feeling defensive.

"He could sense he was losing you, C. It

57

was making him a little crazy," Sherry says, more empathy in her voice than I would like. Fair or not, I want my oldest friend firmly on my side, even if she has been friends with Isaac almost as long. "Ever since we were kids, all he ever wanted was to live happily ever after with you."

"With who he *thought* I was."

"Well, that's all we have, right? Who we think people are?" I can practically hear her shrug. "I guess Isaac kept hoping that if he believed in his version of you long enough and hard enough, you'd start to agree with him, the way I did with Bjorn."

"It's different." Sherry's boyfriend, Bjorn, is the man who finally convinced Sherry that she's worthy of all the hearts and flowers.

Bjorn, a Norwegian pro-surfer who has lived in Maui half his life, thinks Sherry is brilliant, funny, beautiful without makeup, and the sweetest woman on earth. He seems ready to settle down and worship at Sherry's altar, and Sherry feels the same way. I know she treasures the self-love and acceptance Bjorn has helped her find, but Isaac didn't want to help me get in touch with something lovable about myself. He wanted me to change the parts he found unlovable, the unpalatable parts that are nevertheless an undeniable part of who I am.

"I know it's different, but I understand why he kept trying," Sherry says. "He fell hard for you when we were kids, and he hasn't been able to put the old Caitlin to rest the way I have."

"Right." Pain flashes through my chest and I suddenly feel more alone than I have in months. Sherry's never said anything, but I worry that she likes "old Caitlin" better than "new Caitlin," too. When I still had the memory of Gabe's unconditional love and acceptance to fall back on, I didn't let other people's opinions, even my best friends', matter too much, but now...

Now, I'm not sure if Gabe is a fan of "new Caitlin," eithfrer. The look he gave me when he talked about not being "on board" with killing anyone else made me feel like I was going to be sick. I wasn't on board with killing anyone, either. It just...happened. And I dealt with the aftermath as best I could, while carrying the secret all alone.

And now I am still alone, and I will remain that way until the day Gabe remembers the "whys" behind the "whats"—if he ever does.

I push the panic-inducing thought aside. "I'll bring the kids up in about thirty minutes. You want to order Dominos to be delivered to the room?"

"Sure thing," Sherry says. "And hang in there, okay? You and Gabe are going to work things out. Just give him some time to catch up."

"If he wants to catch up," I mumble.

"Stop it," Sherry says. "I refuse to tolerate any negative thinking. Gabe is alive, and you two are going to have your happy ever after, or I swear I'll eat a pound of dog poop."

"Gross." I laugh, but it fades as soon as Emmie comes rushing over to get her hot pink water shooter from the pool bag.

I can't even look at my niece without my stomach knotting. I can't lose Emmie; I can't let Aoife take her away. There has been too much water under the bridge for me to ever trust Aoife with a child I love.

Maybe if she had come back a few months after she left, when Emmie was sick with the flu, and I was home alone, terrified that my six-month-old niece was going to die of dehydration if I couldn't keep fluids in her body. Or if Aoife had come home for Emmie's first birthday, full of apologies, and begging me to go back to high school and complete my senior year one year late. Or maybe if she had just called a *single* damned time between the day she left, and the day she swept back in almost four years later. But she hadn't called. She discarded Emmie like a toy she was tired of playing with, and it had taken her *years* to get around to showing interest in the baby girl she left behind.

Meanwhile, Emmie has grown into an amazing little person who Danny, Ray, and Sean love like a sister, and I would die for in a heartbeat. I love her with every fiber of my being, and I have to believe that kind of love—the kind that stays and loves through the hard times, when loving costs you in blood, sweat, and tears—is worth more than the picture perfect suburban life Aoife is offering.

"Especially since Aoife might get tired of that toy someday, too," I say

"Still talking to yourself, I see."

I sit up fast, spinning to see Gabe standing on the other side of the wrought iron fence surrounding the pool. As soon as my gaze meets his, I am filled with a profound sense of relief. In his eyes, I can see the same regret that has been poisoning my insides for the past few hours, the same longing to make this better, and find a way back to each other, no matter how many roadblocks stand in our way.

"Hey." I stand, crossing the hot concrete in

bare feet, not missing the way his eyes skim up and down my body, making me glad I slipped into my yellow bikini instead of my one-piece swimsuit.

For the first time since my last night with Gabe, electricity courses through my nerve endings making my blood rush and my belly flip and my fingers itch to fist in the course fabric of his white polo and rip it over his head, revealing the beautiful man beneath. I'm suddenly dying for another taste of his lips, for his Gabe smell swirling through my head, and his touch taking me higher than any drug. With just a look, Gabe can make me feel more than Isaac could with his hands all over my body. How could I have ever thought I could settle for less than that? Less than the rush I feel every time I'm in the same time zone as Gabe Alexander.

Gabe's lips part as if he's about to speak, but I don't give him a chance. I close the last few feet between us, take his face in my hands, and pull his lips down to mine. For a moment, I'm aware of the rungs of the metal gate, hot and hard between us, but then there is only Gabe's tongue slipping between my lips, Gabe's fingers driving into my hair, pulling me closer, kissing me with a thoroughness that takes my breath away.

But who needs breath when there is a man who kisses me like I'm the most precious, irreplaceable thing in the world?

I kiss him until my head spins and my belly aches and heat pools between my legs. I kiss him until my hands are shaking and my knees are weak and all I can think about is how much I need to be alone with him.

"I don't want to wait," I whisper against his lips. "I know we should, but I want you too much."

"Should is a stupid word." Gabe's hands fist tighter in my hair, holding me captive as he trails kisses down my throat, where my pulse is racing like a horse set free before a storm. "And waiting is for people who haven't had a year of their lives stolen. I found what I was looking for on my father's computer, by the way."

"Yeah?" My breath rushes out, and I struggle to focus on his words instead of the delicious way he's making me feel.

"It was in his trash," Gabe says, lips moving against my throat as he speaks. "He apparently never empties it. There were files in there from three years ago."

"What did you find?" I let my fingers play through his silky hair, over the scar that is thick and frightening, but beautiful because it is the reason he is alive.

"A memo to his secretary, Charlene, detailing all the things he wanted her to get together for the funeral," Gabe says. "Apparently, they actually held the thing in the back parlor, on the off chance you decided to ignore Dad's letter and show up." He pauses, his breath rushing out over my skin, before he presses another kiss to my cheek. "You were right. My parents are out of their minds. I'm sorry I didn't believe you."

I pull back far enough to look at him, not surprised to see hurt in his eyes. "I understand. And I'm sorry I wasn't more patient. I know it can't be easy learning your parents aren't the people they pretend to be."

Gabe nods ever so slightly and his eyes drop to my lips. "I'd rather not talk about Aaron and Deborah right now, if that's okay."

"What would you like to talk about?"

"I'd prefer not to talk at all," he says, the heat in his voice sending a thrill rushing across my skin. "I'd prefer to take you to my father's office and get my mouth between your legs. I remember that time on the couch, you know."

"You do?" I ask, nipples tightening inside my bikini.

"I remember the way you came on my mouth, with your hands fisted in my hair, pressing my face closer to your body," he says in a soft, silky voice that sends heat rushing between my thighs. "I remember that you tasted like peaches sprinkled with salt and that you let me stay between your legs and stare at your pussy while we talked after. Before I made you come again."

My breath rushes out, but I find I can't think of a thing to say.

"And I remember that yours is the prettiest pussy, my favorite pussy." His thumb trails over my shoulder down my arm, making me shiver. "And I've been dreaming about getting my tongue—"

"Stop." I take a step away from him, not surprised to find I'm trembling. "Don't say another word, or I'm not going to be able to hold it together long enough to get the kids upstairs to the hotel room."

"Holding it together is overrated," Gabe says, that wicked smile on his lips, the same one I remember from all the times he made me beg him for my pleasure before delivering on his promise to make me see stars.

I smile up at him, fighting the urge to lunge for his lips and kiss him senseless all over again. If I start kissing him, I'm not going to stop until our clothes are off and his mouth is warm on my skin and his cock is hot in my hand and we are racing toward the edge of oblivion so fast we're setting the brush at the side of the road on fire.

"Give me five minutes," I say in a husky voice, visions of me and Gabe, naked and entwined, filling my thoughts. "I'll meet you at your car."

"I'm parked right next to the lobby," he says. "And leave the bikini on under your clothes. I want to untie the strings with my teeth."

The words send a rush of desire sweeping through me, and for a second I think I'm going to faint for the second time in my life, only hours after fainting for the first. But instead I laugh, a laugh that is every bit as wicked as the gleam in Gabe's eyes, and spin to rush back to my lounge chair.

I get everyone out of the pool, dried off, and headed up to the room in record time, swinging by the exercise room on the way to tell a still-brooding Danny that supper will be arriving in fifteen to twenty minutes.

"I won't be there, so you'll be free to enjoy your meal," I say. "I'm going out with Gabe."

Danny turns on the weight bench where he's been watching TV, making direct eye contact with me for the first time since we left the wake. "Good. You shouldn't fight with him, Caitlin. He's the only person who's always been on our side, no matter what. You know that. He's got your back like nobody else."

"I know," I say, not ready to tell Danny that Gabe doesn't remember everything about the night he saved my life, or necessarily approve of how far we went in the name of protecting the people we cared about.

Danny and I have never discussed that night in detail, but he suspects that Gabe and I killed Pitt, and I know it would upset him if he thought Gabe wasn't the same Gabe anymore. Danny hated Gabe at first, but by the end of last summer, my brother had a pretty decent case of hero worship going where my boyfriend was concerned. Gabe wasn't your typical role model, but I figured Danny could do worse than idolizing a man who would do anything to protect the people he loves.

After this afternoon, I have hope that, with a little help, Gabe might be that man again very soon.

A LOVE SO DEEP

CHAPTER
Six

Gabe

"I have seen a medicine
That's able to breathe life into a stone."
-Shakespeare

Visions of all the times Caitlin and I were naked together dance in front of my eyes as I guide the Beamer through the sleepy Sunday streets of downtown Giffney, headed for my father's office. I'm embarrassed to admit it, but of all the things I've remembered about Caitlin so far, our time in bed has returned with the most clarity.

"I can't remember your birthday, but I remember fucking you in seven different positions," I confess, because I've decided to be honest with her, even when it's embarrassing, even when it's hard. Realizing my parents are such accomplished liars made me determined to excel at telling the truth.

Caitlin shifts in her seat as she turns to face me, causing the jean skirt she pulled on over her suit to ride up her tan thighs, and my blood pressure to spike. "It's April tenth, the night we ran into each other at the club."

The words trigger a chain reaction in my brain, like dominos toppling in a line, and I suddenly remember. "We were dancing, and then you ran away...but I followed you and started talking to Sherry. She said it was your birthday, but you weren't in the mood to party because..."

I trail off, heart beating faster with excitement as more memories flood in. "That's why we robbed that pawnshop. So you and the kids could keep the house."

"Yes!" She reaches out, squeezing my leg through my shorts, her excitement obvious in the way her fingers dig into my skin. "All the robberies were like that, Gabe. We robbed the people we found in your father's old files, people who deserved to be in jail for the horrible things they'd done."

"And we put the money in your college

fund," I say. "Have you—"

"I've already finished a year of my degree in social work," she says pride in her voice. "I'm hoping to finish in another two years."

I smile. "So you decided to go for the big money career, huh?"

"You know it," she says, with a chuckle. "But seriously, I don't need that much money to be happy, and I like the idea of helping kids that are in situations like the one I was in growing up. I certainly know what it's like to be in their shoes."

I glance at her, hating myself for being so quick to judge her this afternoon. I should have known better. "I'm proud of you."

"Don't be too proud. I haven't graduated yet, and I've had...other things keeping me busy. Things I'm not so sure..." She trails off and her fingers tangle in her lap, the way they do when she's nervous. I remember that. I'm remembering so much more quickly now that Caitlin is back in my life.

"Tell me, please," I urge. "This is helping me remember."

She sighs and glances down at her hands. "This isn't about our history together, but you should probably know..." She looks back up and I feel her watching me as I take a left toward my father's office. "I've been pulling jobs on the island, helping people in impossible situations."

The phrase sparks something in my brain. "Impossible situations?"

"That's what you said to me on my birthday last year," she says. "That none of us know what we're capable of until we find ourselves in an impossible situation. A situation that makes us think about the best way to use the time we've been given." She pauses, adding in a softer voice as I pull into the parking lot behind my father's office, "I remember the first night we came here. It seems like so much more than a year ago."

I guide the Beamer into my father's reserved space and shut off the car, but I don't unbuckle my belt or move to get out. "So you've been stealing from people?"

She nods, but she doesn't look at me. Her eyes are on the red door that leads up to my father's second story office. "Just a few people so far. One man owed years of back child support, and another was blackmailing a woman into continuing their affair. The people they were hurting were in impossible situations and I guess..." She shifts her gaze, a naked look in her eyes that makes me want to pull her into my arms and kiss the furrow from between her brows. "I guess I was in an impossible situation, too."

I thread my fingers through hers, waiting for her to continue.

"Trying to move on with my life without you was…so hard," she says, a catch in her voice. "So much has happened. Awful things I should tell you, but I just…can't right now. I'm not ready."

"We agreed we don't like the word should." I lift her hand to my lips and press a kiss to her soft skin. "Tell me when you're ready. But I want you to know that I realize I was an asshole this afternoon. I'm in no place to judge anyone or anything. I'm stuck between who I was, who I thought I was, and who I want to be. I don't know how everything is going to shake out, but I know I want to be with you when it does."

"Me too," she says, eyes shimmering with emotion. "I want that more than anything."

"But I'm going to be honest with you," I say. "I fucked about half of the town this summer. Any blonde between the ages of eighteen and twenty-eight who would let me follow her home from the bar."

Caitlin's lips curve on one side in an unexpected smile. "Well, that's very…you. Old you. Before me." She narrows her eyes. "I hope you were careful."

"Wrapped up tighter than a Cuban cigar every time," I say with a grin that fades quickly. "But none of them meant anything to me. Only one was even a friend, and it never got more serious than that. I called her this afternoon to tell her it was over."

"So you're fresh from a breakup," she says, brows drifting higher on her forehead.

"It wasn't like that. She was a place to hide, not a place to find the things I've been missing."

Caitlin nods, the tenderness in her expression making it clear she understands. But then, she seems to understand me better than anyone, maybe even better than I understand myself.

"I was with someone, too," she says. "Isaac and I were living together until a few days ago."

The way she says the name makes it clear I should remember this person, but I don't. "Isaac is…an old boyfriend? Before us?"

Caitlin blinks before she shakes her head. "Sorry, I forget. No, Isaac is an old friend from Giffney. You two met once. Big guy, very protective of me?" I shake my head, indicating the description still isn't ringing a bell, and she continues with a shrug. "It doesn't matter, but I think you liked him.

Anyway…Isaac followed me to Maui a couple of months after the kids and I left. Eventually we became a couple, but I never loved him the way he deserved to be loved. I broke things off right before we flew back for the funeral. I couldn't live that…half life anymore."

I make a considering sound, fighting to keep the spark of jealousy in my chest from catching fire. "So you're fresh from a breakup, too."

"Not really. Isaac will make someone a great husband someday, but for me…" She lifts one bare shoulder. "It was like you said, he was a place to hide. And I was tired of hiding."

A shadow flickers across her face and I suddenly know what she's not telling me. It is an instinctive knowing, a limb tingling as it sinks beneath cool water, something I couldn't ignore any more than I could ignore my own arm or leg.

"You don't have to hide anymore." I stare deep into her eyes, willing her to see that I'm ready for her, all of her. "Don't hold back with me. I want you to be exactly who you are, and if I can't handle it, then I'm the one who's failed, not you."

"That's not true," she says. "People change,

I know that. It doesn't mean anyone has failed."

I shake my head. "It does for me. I realized something this afternoon, when I found that memo in my father's office. Ever since the surgery, I've been afraid of myself. I thought I was afraid of my dark side, but I'm not. I'm afraid I won't have the guts to become the person I need to be, the person I obviously was when I met you."

"What do you mean?" she asks, brow furrowing again.

"My parents have played with our lives like our free will doesn't matter. We've been pieces in their chess game," I say, rage and betrayal rising inside me all over again, the way they did when I sat in front of my father's computer this afternoon. "I come from people who prove there's no point in playing by the rules. There will always be someone bigger and stronger, with more power, and no moral compass, who refuses to do the right thing. And those people make it ludicrous to think decent people can walk the straight and narrow and expect the world not to go to hell in a hand basket."

I swallow. "Deep down, I knew that sometimes you have to play dirty to make sure the bad guys don't win, but until today, I was ignoring the signs, wanting to stay out of the shadows. Wanting things to be…easy."

"I don't think life is ever easy," Caitlin says, laying her hand on top of mine. "But love can be."

I look at her beautiful face and my heart flips in my chest and I no longer feel like a person who's gotten the short end of the stick. I feel like the luckiest bastard in the world, because she's talking about me, and there is a place in her heart that is mine.

I lean in, pressing a grateful kiss to her lips before resting my forehead against hers. "Thank you."

"You don't have to thank me…but there is something I would like."

"Anything," I say, meaning it.

"Take me inside," she whispers.

I reach for my door—not needing to be asked twice—but she stops me with a hand on my arm. "But not the couch," she says. "I want a new memory, without any ghosts in it."

I nod, already knowing exactly where I'll take her. To a place where I can watch the setting sun turn her tawny skin gold as I kiss every inch of her body, until she's begging me to do more than kiss, and I sink inside her, and finally find out if real life can compare to all the dreams I've had of her.

Dreams of being shattered and made whole, dreams of finding everything I've ever wanted in one beautiful girl's arms.

CHAPTER
Seven

Caitlin

"I love you not only for what you are,
but for what I am when I am with you."
-Elizabeth Barrett Browning

We go in through the red door and head up the long staircase hand in hand. It's lighter than it was the last time Gabe and I crept into his father's office on a Sunday. The sunset light filters in through the window at the top of the stairs, turning the air a rosy gold that makes even a law office seem like the perfect setting for a romantic reunion.

I see the leather couch in the corner has been replaced by a larger couch with carved arms made of blond wood covered in striped canvas, and think maybe it would have been okay to make a memory there, after all, but Gabe doesn't pause on his way through the room. He leads me through the office into the small bathroom, where he opens a crystalized window to reveal a metal fire escape.

"The roof okay?" He glances back at me, heat and caution mixing on his handsome face, making it clear I'm not the only one who's feeling as anxious as I am eager.

Will making love with him feel the way it used to? Or will it be like being with someone new? I have no idea, and I'm not sure it matters, as long as it is wild and raw and sweet.

"The roof is perfect." I follow him out onto the fire escape, and up the metal rungs leading to the top of the four-story building. It's the tallest building on the block, so no curious neighbors will be spying on us, and I can't remember the last time I saw a helicopter fly over Giffney. I feel certain we'll have privacy if not comfort, but then we step over the concrete ledge at the top of the fire escape, and my worries about hot tar beneath my back vanish in a rush of delight.

"It's beautiful," I breathe, drifting across the roof to the garden on the other side.

Raised beds full of white daisies and violet verbena stand at right angles, surrounding a set of table and chairs, and two loungers with thick red cushions. Strings of bare bulbs crisscross overhead, and a stereo and grill stand in the shelter of a wooden cabana that hints at the gatherings that must have been held here.

"Charlene did all of this," Gabe says, coming to stand next to me as I lean down to smell the verbena. "She and her husband come up here every Friday night. They've been married for twenty years, but still can't get enough of each other."

The mention of Charlene's name is like someone flipped a dimmer, muting the golden evening. I stand, the lemon scent of the verbena leaving an astringent taste in my mouth. "I remember meeting her when I came to pick you up after work. She seemed so nice…" I shake my head, hating that the dark things have followed us up here, to this refuge from the world. "Why would she help your parents fake your funeral? Did she have any idea why they were doing what they did?"

"I don't know," Gabe says. "We'll search her desk before we go, but right now I have more important things to do."

He wraps his arms around my waist, pulling

my back to his front, sending awareness coursing through me as our bodies slide into place, fitting together as perfectly as we always have. He presses a kiss to my neck, my jaw, the hollow beneath my ear, before he captures my earlobe between his teeth and bites down hard enough to make me suck in a breath through my teeth.

"Still like biting?" he asks, fingers digging into my hips.

"Still like biting." My pulse speeds and my nipples pull tight, celebrating the feel of his teeth raking across my skin.

He fists his hand in the hair at the base of my neck, forcing my head back as his lips return to my throat. "How about this?"

"Yes," I moan, eyes sliding closed as my muscles go limp and my knees start to feel decidedly weak. I arch back against Gabe, until his erection pushes against the small of my back, making me shiver. He feels so perfect, the size and shape of him as familiar as my own face in the mirror, even after all this time apart.

"And what about getting fucked like I mean it?" he asks, the hitch in his voice making the course words sweeter than any of the endearments Isaac whispered into my ear.

My ribs contract and my heart lurches and I

suddenly feel like I'm going to start crying the way I did when I saw Gabe's face this morning, because he *remembers*. He remembers that last night, when there was nothing but him and me, and all the horrible, wonderful longing for more time, more love, more everything we were to each other. He may not remember every moment we shared, but he remembers that heartbreaking, soul-healing night, and right now that is enough.

"You always fuck me like you mean it." I turn in his arms, twining my arms around his neck, echoing his response when I'd begged him to take me harder, to fuck me like it was the last, best thing either of us would ever do.

"Don't be gentle," I say, standing on tiptoe, kissing him with the words. "I don't want gentle tonight."

He curses beneath his breath, letting me know I drive him as crazy as he drives me. "I don't think I could hold back right now. Even if I tried."

"Don't try," I whisper, a startled sound escaping my throat as he swings me into his arms, sweeping me off my feet so swiftly my head is still spinning when he lies me down on the lounge chair and covers my body with his own.

Our lips meet in a bruising kiss that is a

frenzied tangle of lips, teeth, and tongues, not even close to the languid kisses we usually start with. But Gabe's right—tonight, a slow burn would be impossible. Right now, we are a spark and kindling catching fire, igniting with enough heat to burn down the entire building.

His hands work their magic and suddenly my skirt and tank top are gone, without me remembering shifting to help him make them disappear. And then he's pulling away from me to rip his shirt over his head, revealing chiseled muscles sharper and more defined than the toned chest I remember.

"Become a meathead while I've been gone?" I ask, hands shaking as I trail my fingers down his rounded pecs, to the taut ridges of his abdomen.

He was lovely before, but now he is…perfection, so gorgeous it seems a shame sculpting the male figure went out of vogue with the ancient Greeks. Someone should sculpt this man, immortalize every inch of his beauty in marble for women to drool over for generations to come.

"You know I enjoy torturing myself," he says, a pained expression flickering across his face as I hook my fingers over the waistband of his shorts.

"No torture tonight, only good things." I dip my hand lower, raking my fingernails over the bulge straining his fly, drawing another curse from his lips.

He captures my wrists in his hands, drawing my arms up over my head before pinning them to the lounge chair's cushions. "Not yet. If I take any more clothes off, I'll be inside you in thirty seconds."

"You say that like it's a bad thing." I wrap my legs around his waist, flexing my muscles until I've pinned his hips to mine. His cock presses against me through his shorts and my thin bikini bottom, making my entire body tighten with desire.

"I'm not the only one who's changed." He runs his hands from my knees to my thighs before giving them a squeeze. "Run any marathons lately?"

"I don't do organized athletic activity. I run at night, by myself." I punctuate the words with circles of my hips, grinding against him through our clothes. "I run so I'll be fast enough to get away from the bad guys."

"You are so fucking sexy," Gabe says, breath shuddering out against my lips as his palms slide higher, until his fingers nearly encircle my waist.

He dips his head with a growl, finding the

end of the bikini strap tied around my neck with his teeth and loosening the bow with a jerk of his head. My top springs free, baring my breasts, and a moment later Gabe is pulling my nipple into his mouth. Immediately, I forget that I was going to tell him that he is sexier, and that I'm never going to get enough of his body.

I forget everything but the amazing way he makes me feel.

CHAPTER

eight

Caitlin

Waves of bliss course from my breast to every electrified inch of my skin until I'm moaning and squirming beneath him. I thread my fingers through his hair and try to tug his mouth away from my chest, but he only intensifies his efforts, licking and sucking and biting until my breasts ache and the flesh between my legs is swollen and slick. I feel bruised with wanting him, and I only crave more. More of his kiss, his touch, more of the way he makes me feel like my skin is too small and my soul too big for this fragile human body.

"Please." My fingers claw into his thick biceps, so much denser than they used to be.

"I don't want to wait. I need you. Now."

"Not yet," he mumbles against my breast, but a moment later, his hand slips beneath my bikini bottom and his fingers slide through where I am hot and wet and dying for the relief I know only he can give me.

"God, Caitlin." He groans as he kisses his way down my ribs until his breath warms my fluttering belly. "You taste so good. I don't want to be able to taste anything but you."

I whimper. I want to tell him I need him inside me, where I have craved him so desperately that I wake from dreams of the two of us with tears streaming down my cheeks. But before I can form the words, he's made my bikini bottom vanish and hooked my knees over his shoulders. And then he lowers his mouth between my legs and I remember that there is something almost as good as Gabe's cock.

His mouth.

God, his mouth.

His tongue teases through my heat, sending more blood rushing between my legs as he circles my clit with the perfect, delicious pressure. He takes me right up to the very edge, close enough that I can feel the hot winds of oblivion blowing across my cheeks, promising to sweep me away to a world where there is nothing but bliss, before Gabe abruptly abandons his work.

I suck in a ragged breath, but before my moan of frustration can escape my lips, Gabe drives his tongue inside me, wrenching a different kind of cry from my throat. He drives in and out, fucking me with his tongue as his hands hook around my thighs and spread me wide, wider, until I am completely exposed.

But I know this is how he likes it. He loves me like this, laid open to him, hiding nothing, concealing nothing, shamelessly reaching for the pleasure he wants to give me. I buck into him until every muscle in my body is strung tight, and my breath is coming fast enough to make me dizzy. I fist my hands in the cushion above my head, desperate to have something to hang on to, and then it happens.

Gabe tips me over the edge and I'm falling, spinning weightlessly through the air as my womb contracts and my toes curl and my features twist with the horrible beauty of it all. I make a face I know isn't pretty, but I don't try to hide when Gabe surges up over me, bringing his lips back to mine.

I let my breath rush out into his mouth, tasting my taste on his lips, clinging to his shoulders as he disposes of his shorts and boxers with one swift movement. I hear the tearing of foil and feel Gabe's hands moving between our bodies as he sheaths himself and then the hot, pulsing head of him is at my entrance and he's pushing inside.

He drives home with a savage thrust and a groan that is wild and primal and makes my teeth ache with the need to trap flesh between them and bite down. He pushes in and in and in, until every inch of him is buried inside me, and the head of him butts up against the end of me.

I throw back my head, squeeze my eyes closed, and cry out, just that one single thrust almost enough to take me over again, but then Gabe pulls back, depriving me of all that sweet fullness.

"Look at me." He cups my face in his hands, his voice as ragged as my soul feels. "I need to see your eyes."

I look up at him, into him, and at that moment—with both of our walls down, and nothing but skin on skin, and sweat, and blood pumping too fast between us—I see everything. I see down to the heart of him, and I know that none of the other bullshit matters. He is Gabe, and he is mine, and I am his, and I am going to love him forever. I am going to love him until I die, and after.

Looking into his eyes, I believe in reincarnation, because one lifetime isn't enough time to love this man. I need forever, eternity.

"I love you." I know it's too soon, but this moment is too real for secrets.

"I love you," he says, throat working as he swallows. "I thought I needed the memories, but...all I need is you. You're all I'll ever need."

Tears fill my eyes, but I press my lips together, fighting through the emotion, not wanting to cry. Right now, I just want to be with him, and for our second first time to last forever.

As if he's read my mind—and maybe he has, the same way he's read my heart—Gabe's second thrust is infinitely slower than his first. He glides into me with a long, languid stroke as he moves his hands beneath my back to cup my ass in his hands. He shifts my hips until we hit that sweet spot where every thrust takes me a little closer to bliss, and then he sets about driving me slowly out of my mind.

With Isaac, slow meant slow and steady, a long distance runner plodding resolutely toward the finish line. With Gabe, slow is a roller coaster creeping toward the apex, making my stomach flip and my thighs tremble and my heart lodge in my throat because I know the fall is coming. I know it's coming and it will be epic and terrifying and wonderful and I will never be the same after he takes me there.

There...there...closer...closer...

"Yes," I gasp, fingers digging into the back of his neck, breath coming fast against his lips as he drives home and my body quivers like a bow string about to break. "Yes. Please, Gabe, now."

"Come for me, Caitlin," he breathes. "Come for me."

And I do, the way I always do with him, my body obeying his command like I was made to lie beneath him, made to spread my legs and lift my hips and come, crying out his name, as his rhythm grows faster and he takes me with all the passion we create together. He comes moments after I do, his cock pulsing inside of me, sending aftershocks of his pleasure echoing through my bones. I swear I can feel how good it is for him, like part of my soul is tangled up in his.

It's so much more than an orgasm. It's a celebration, a prayer of thanksgiving for the return of lost things. He whispers that he loves me again, but I don't need to hear the words, I can feel the truth in the way he holds me close and kisses me like I am the answer to every question, the balm for every hurt, the only thing in his world that could never be replaced.

After, we lie tangled together, catching our breath as the sun sets and the air begins to cool. My fingertips drift up and down his back, relishing every brush of skin against skin, the miracle of him, of this moment, of *us*, too big for words.

"Let's stay here forever," he says, hugging me closer, kissing my bare shoulder.

"Okay," I agree with a content sigh. "We can hang hammocks and go to sleep watching the stars every night."

"Sounds like heaven."

"Until it rains." I kiss his cheek.

"Or the mosquitoes descend."

"We'll get mosquito coils," I say. "We have tons of mosquitoes at the house in Hawaii, but with a few coils burning, we can hang out without getting devoured. Except Emmie, the poor thing. Mosquitoes love her. I tell her it must be because she's sweeter than the rest of us."

He props up on his forearms, smiling down at me. "I don't know, you're pretty sweet."

"As sweet as you remember?"

"Sweeter." He traces the curve of my ear

with a fingertip, even that innocent touch enough to make my body start humming all over again. "I should get rid of the condom, but then I want to hear about Hawaii. How you got there, where you live, where you go to school, whether you've learned to surf...everything. I want to feel like I've been there with you."

I smile, feeling like the luckiest woman in the world, as I watch my gorgeous man walk naked across the roof to toss the used condom in a trashcan near the grill, and turn back to me with a smile on his face that assures me there is nowhere he'd rather be than here with me.

After we're snuggled up again, I tell him about Aunt Sarah and the will, about flying out with the kids. I tell him about Danny's girlfriend, Sam, and how well he's been doing in school. I tell him about the friends I've made at the community pool, and the way Emmie took to swimming like she was born in the water. I tell him about my courses at the U of H, Maui campus, and my night runs, and how sometimes the sadness was so strong nothing could make me feel better except running down to the shore and watching the waves pound against the rocks.

And then, finally, I tell him about the baby.

How, at first, knowing I was having our child was all that kept me going, and how losing that sweet little life almost killed me. I can't keep from crying as I confess it all, but it's okay, because Gabe cries, too. He pulls me into his arms and wraps himself around me and my tears wet his chest and his tears dampen my hair, but for the first time, the grief is bearable, because Gabe is here to share it with me.

By the time we're finished talking and crying and talking some more, the sun has long set and the first stars are flickering to life in the dark blue sky, but we still don't move for a long time. We stay entwined on the lounge chair, quiet in the darkness, giving everything we've shared time to settle and harden, cementing us to each other even tighter than we were before, so tight I know nothing will ever come between us again.

"We're going to take care of the things that need to be taken care of, and then we're getting out of here," Gabe says, proving he feels it, too, that he and I have become *us* again. "I'm coming to Hawaii with you. I'm not going back to my old school. I'll finish up what I can on Maui, and then take things from there."

"I think the campus on Oahu has a law

school," I say. "We could rent out the Maui house, and move islands when you get in."

He hugs me closer. "You've got a lot of faith in me."

"Absolutely," I say, pressing a kiss to his bare chest.

"I can't believe I left to go have the surgery without at least trying to contact you," he says, confirming my suspicion that this is the part of our story that troubles him the most. "Something must have happened. Something with my parents." He curses. "I wish I could fucking remember."

"You will," I say, believing it with my entire heart. "So much has come back to you, just today. Give it time."

"It's already taken too much time," he says. "I hate that I wasn't there for you. I hate that I don't know why my parents did what they did."

"Then let's go see what we can find," I say, standing and stretching my arms over my head, feeling more satisfied than I've felt in ages. "I'll take Charlene's computer, and you see what you can find on your father's."

"Sounds perfect," he says, smacking my bare bottom, making me laugh as I turn to retaliate, chasing him naked across the roof to smack his ass before we declare a truce and walk hand in hand back to reclaim our clothes.

Minutes later, we're dressed and headed back down the fire escape to Aaron Alexander's office, ready to hunt for the answers we need to put the past to rest and get started on forever.

CHAPTER
Nine

Gabe

"Come what sorrow can,
It cannot countervail the exchange of joy,
That one short minute gives me in her sight."
-Shakespeare

Every minute with her is more perfect than the last. It doesn't matter if we're talking, making love, goofing off, or hacking into computers on opposite sides of a quiet law office, every second with Caitlin confirms that this is where I'm supposed to be.

I understand now why, since coming home from the surgery, I've felt like a guest at Darby Hill. Darby Hill isn't my home, my home is five feet, one inches of hard-working, hard-loving, fearless, fragile, beautiful blonde and I never want to leave that home again.

"I'm not going back to Darby Hill tonight," I say, gazing across the office to where Caitlin sits cross-legged in Charlene's chair, clicking through her email. "I won't be able to resist the urge to strangle my parents."

Caitlin doesn't say a word, and I've started to think she hasn't heard me when she says—

"We can't go back to Hawaii, either." Her voice is trembling, and I know she's found something bad, even before I cross the room to stand beside her and she looks up at me, a haunted expression on her face. She points to the screen in front of her. "Look at this."

I lean down, rubbing her back in gentle circles as I read through a series of emails between Charlene and two lawyers on the island of Maui. She solicited them to assist her in transferring a property to "a deserving young family" who would only accept the property if it seemed to come to them through the will of a dead relative. I read the entire string of messages, but I realize by the third response from Sumiko and Associates what has happened.

"My parents bought you the house in Maui," I say. "To make sure there were a few thousand miles and an ocean between us."

Caitlin's breath rushes out. "And you were right. My dad was in on it. They paid him ten grand to help them pull off the inheritance story, and get me out of town. I found an email Charlene wrote to him before I found this one, but it didn't mention anything about why they were offering the money, or why he'd agree to it."

I brush her hair over her shoulder. "Are you going to be okay?"

Her cheeks puff as she blows out a long stream of air. "I mean…my dad is breaking my heart all over again, even though he's dead, and the kids and I are homeless, but…"

"You're not homeless." I urge her up out of the chair before taking her place, and pulling her into my lap. "The house is in your name. There's no reason you can't keep living there."

"It feels tainted now." She curls into me, wrapping her arms around my neck, allowing me to comfort her in a way that makes me feel like the luckiest man alive. I never imagined being there for someone could feel like a gift instead of a responsibility.

I also never dreamed it would be so devastating to learn I was almost a father.

The thought makes my stomach turn to

lead, so I push it away, even as I hold Caitlin closer. I can't think about how things might have been different—if Caitlin and I had been allowed to stay together, if she'd been there for me after the surgery, and I'd been there for her during the pregnancy. I can't imagine a scenario where our child lived without wanting to kill my parents for what they've done more than I do already.

"Finding answers sucks," Caitlin says, reaching out to click the browser closed.

"But we still have one very big question left."

"Why did they go to all this trouble," Caitlin says, completing my thought with an ease that is more evidence that we belong together. "All told, this deception must have cost almost a million dollars."

"And even to my parents, that's not a small number." I hum a tune I can't put words to, but for the first time since the surgery, the hole in my memory doesn't bother me. I recovered the most important part of who I used to be, and she is threading her fingers through my hair, twisting it in idle circles as she thinks.

"Your mom was angry with me," Caitlin says. "She said she only put up with having me around because she hoped I would convince you to have the surgery, but that she should have known better. She said she never should have trusted a girl who could fall in love with the heartless person you'd become. She thought the tumor had changed you, made you...ruthless and cold. I think those were the words she used."

I grunt. "Amusing that she could accuse someone else of being ruthless with a straight face."

Caitlin turns to me, her brow furrowed. "But she did. And she was really upset. She was crying her eyes out, just...shattered. I never doubted for a second that you were really dead, not until Sherry started trying to find out where you were being buried, and the pieces didn't add up."

"So I'm guessing getting me on the plane to Michigan wasn't an easy job."

Caitlin's frown deepens. "They might have drugged you or something."

"Seems extreme, but after learning they dumped half a million dollars on a house in Hawaii..." I curl my fingers into Caitlin's hip as I turn the chair away from the desk to face the window, where the moon is rising. "But I still have no idea why. They could have kidnapped me, and taken me to the clinic, but the doctors wouldn't have operated without my consent. And why would I give consent in a situation like that, without at least calling you first?"

She shakes her head. "I don't know, but until we do, you need to stay away from Darby Hill. And we have to make sure your parents don't know the kids and I are in town. I was considering having the kids skip the funeral anyway, because it will be so upsetting, but now I'm definitely having them stay with Sherry."

"What about you?" I ask. "My parents know what you look like."

She curses. "I know. And with your dad being so big in the law community, I don't know how I'm going to find a lawyer to represent me without him finding out about it."

"We'll hire someone from Charleston if it comes time to lawyer up," I say. "But I've been thinking about this thing with your sister, and I think we should make sure we've exhausted all our options first. A woman with her history must have a few skeletons in her closet she won't want the court finding out about."

Caitlin's cocks her head, shooting me a look out of the corner of her eye. "So you think we should do recon? Look into this perfect new life in Florida? See if we can find any holes in her story?"

"I do, and I think you should skip the funeral. My parents were acting very interested in whether or not I planned to attend. They may come by to check on the festivities."

"I'll go get a hat with a veil tomorrow morning, or something to cover my hair and face," she says. "No matter how mad I am at Chuck right now…he was my dad, and I don't want to miss his funeral. At the end, he was sorry for what he did."

"Too little, too late," I say, having no empathy for anyone involved in this deception.

"Not really. I might not have come back for the funeral if it hadn't been for the emails he sent. But your parents aren't sorry, Gabe. I want you to be careful."

"You're afraid they're dangerous." I clench my jaw, the thought of my parents ripping Caitlin and me apart again making me want to pack our bags and leave Giffney tonight.

"I *know* they're dangerous," she says. "Do you have anywhere you could tell them you're going where they won't ask questions? A friend's house, or something?"

I shake my head. "I'll just get a room at the

hotel where you're staying."

"Okay, but you'll need a story to tell your parents, and we'll have to park your car somewhere else," she says. "Just in case they decide to check on you. Surely you have someone you can count on to keep a secret, or who will at least let you park your car in their driveway."

I make a face, because there is only one person I can think of, and I burned that bridge on the way to Caitlin's hotel.

"What?" she asks, a smile teasing the edges of her lips. "Is it a girl?"

I shrug, and Caitlin laughs.

"Call her. If you were really just friends, she might still be cool."

"And you'd be cool with that?" I ask, lifting a brow.

"I'm cool with anything that keeps you safe, and with me." She kisses me and I know it's true. I can feel it in the way her tongue teases across my top lip before slipping into my mouth, in the way she melts against me when I pull her closer. She knows I belong to her, body and soul.

"Just call her," she says, kissing me between the words. "Then we can go get the rental van from the hotel, and get things taken care of before it gets too late."

I pull reluctantly away from her addictive lips. "I'll call now. She lives in an apartment building, and they clean the streets every few days. I'll have to drop off the keys so she can move the car if she needs to."

"Perfect," Caitlin says. "And if we hurry, we'll still have time to christen the bed in your new hotel room when we get back."

I'm up and out of the chair with my phone to my ear in seconds, the chance to get Caitlin in a bed more than enough motivation to get my ass in gear.

CHAPTER
Ten

Caitlin

Gabe's fuck buddy answers on the second ring and seems eager to help which is partly a relief, and partly…worrisome.

I have a hard time believing this woman would be so amenable if there weren't more emotions on her side than Gabe's. Still, I decide to go with him to hand over the keys. It would be less awkward for me to stay in the van, but I don't want to let Gabe out of my sight. I realize I'm being paranoid, but I just got him back. I don't want to risk him disappearing on me again.

I park the van behind Gabe's Beamer and join him on the sidewalk, slipping my hand into his as the door to the apartment building opens, and two pretty women dressed in jean shorts and tank tops step out. One is tall, with stick straight brown hair to her waist, and clever brown eyes that look familiar. I've met her at least once, though I can't pinpoint where, but I know immediately that the brunette isn't Gabe's girl. His is the petite blonde, with the big blue eyes, the one, who except for the eye color, natural kink in her hair, and *much* bigger boobs, could easily be my twin.

My jaw drops. The resemblance is that uncanny, and I know the other girl sees it, too. She does a double take and casts a meaningful look at her friend, who makes a vaguely disgusted sound I know is intended for Gabe's ears.

"Hello, Kimmy," Gabe says with a smile, apparently the only one who doesn't feel intensely awkward. "This is Caitlin. Caitlin, Kimmy."

"Nice to meet you," I say, though it certainly isn't. At all.

"You too," Kimmy says, but her eyes barely flicker in my direction before she turns back to her friend. "This is Mona. She just started working at the bar. We were headed out for late night pizza when you called."

"What's up?" Mona lifts her chin, but doesn't extend a hand. She obviously isn't thrilled to be in the middle of this, and I can't say I blame her. I wish I'd stayed in the van and never met Kimmy, or her intimidating chest.

"Here are the keys," Gabe says, holding them out to Kimmy. "Feel free to drive the car if you want. I know sometimes the Chevy isn't the most reliable mode of transportation."

Kimmy takes the keys, her fingers caressing Gabe's for a split second that is nevertheless long enough to make me nauseous. "Cool. Thanks. Oh, and I have a few of your things upstairs. I boxed them up. Should I go get them, or—"

"If the door's unlocked, I can go," Gabe says, moving past her before I can make eye contact and silently beg him not to leave me alone.

"Sure, go ahead." Kimmy waves a slender arm covered in silver bracelets. "That way you can check for anything I might have missed. The box is next to the door."

"Be right back." Gabe shoots me a smile I don't return before he turns and practically sprints up the stairs. I appreciate his effort to be hasty, but I would have rather avoided being left to make conversation with the girl he was fucking, and her friend.

"You're Caitlin Cooney, right?" Mona asks, confirming we must know each other.

"I am," I say, forcing a smile. "But I'm sorry, I don't remember where we've met."

"It's okay. It was only once, at Frank's Pies, when you came in to say goodbye to Isaac." She shrugs. "I work part time in the kitchen. I only remember you because Isaac left to go live with you not too long after, and his mom hasn't shut up about it since." She glances over her shoulder and turns back with an arched brow. "But I guess you and Isaac aren't together anymore? So maybe he'll be moving back?"

"Um, no, we're not together," I say, cursing my bad luck. I *would* run into someone who knows Isaac. "But I don't think he plans to move back. He's working for the Maui police department, and really enjoys his job."

"A cop." Kimmy blinks her big blue eyes. "That's quite a switch from Gabe, huh?"

I pull a face, pretending I have no idea what she's talking about, even as I wonder how much Gabe has told her about how we used to be together.

"You know, he's not exactly your typical nice guy," Kimmy says. "But he's been through a lot. It was hard on him, going through surgery alone."

I feel the barb in the words, but I'm not about to defend myself. Not to her, not after everything Gabe and I have been through, so I just shrug and say, "Life's been hard for a lot of people this past year."

"Don't I know it." Kimmy nods, the accusing expression on her face making it clear she's not ready to let this go. "I've been there when Gabe wakes up screaming. It's not pretty."

"Well, you won't have to deal with that anymore," I say sweetly, a barb in my words this time, one that I know both women hear.

Mona shifts her weight uncomfortably, as if she's worried a short blond girl fight is about to break out on the sidewalk, but I have no intention of lifting a finger against Kimmy. She's helping Gabe, and Gabe didn't know I was alive when they were together. I have no animosity toward this woman. I just want to get rid of Gabe's keys, and get back to a place where we can be alone. I'll hold him when he wakes up screaming tonight, and every night, for the rest of our lives if I have to. But I have a feeling neither of us will be suffering through those kinds of dreams anymore. Our nightmare is over.

Or almost over, as soon as we get to the bottom of the mystery with his parents, and get the hell out of South Carolina.

"Thanks for helping Gabe out," I say, in an attempt to defuse the situation. "We both appreciate it."

"Of course," Kimmy says. "I'm here whenever he needs me."

The fact that *I* am excluded from this transaction in her mind is obvious, but I don't care. By helping Gabe, she's helping me, whether she wants to or not.

Gabe hurries out the door a moment later with a box in his arms. His breath is coming fast, making it clear he did his best to hurry, and the concern in his eyes banishes any irritation I felt at being abandoned. We bid Mona and Kimmy a quick good-bye and head back toward the van, while the two women hurry down the street, clearly equally eager to end our meeting.

I walk down the sidewalk beside Gabe, stealing a glance into the box, which appears to contain male toiletries, a few tee shirts, and a couple of pairs of boxer shorts. No cell phone charger, or iPad, two things I know Gabe wouldn't be without if he had ever stayed over for more than a night or two at a time.

"Sorry about that," he says. "I thought it would be faster if I went upstairs. Kimmy's not the sort to get in a hurry."

"Neither is Isaac," I say with a sniff, not saying a word when Gabe hip checks me as we reach the van.

"I thought you weren't jealous," he says, leaning against the passenger's door.

I cross my arms. "That was before I saw my twin with the gigantic boobs."

Gabe frowns. "Twin? She looks nothing like you."

"You've got to be kidding," I snort.

"I'm not," he says, sounding confused. "You're a thousand times prettier, and your breasts are the most beautiful breasts I've ever seen. They're the perfect size, the perfect shape, and only slightly less stunning than your pussy."

I roll my eyes, but I can't keep from grinning, because I can tell he means every word. "Fine, but you're an idiot if you can't see the similarities."

"I'm not an idiot." He leans into me, brushing a kiss across my forehead. "I'm very clever, and forward-thinking, except when it comes to other people we've slept with. That just makes me sad, so I'd rather not talk about that any more, if that's all right."

"It's better than all right," I say, grin slipping. "I wish there hadn't been anyone else. I wish I'd never been with anyone but you."

"Me too," he says, setting the box on the edge of the sidewalk and reaching for me. "I've never done it right with anyone else, anyway."

"What do you mean?" I come into his arms, hooking my wrists behind his neck, marveling all over again that we fit so perfectly together.

"It should mean something…everything," he says, sending warmth spreading through my chest. "After tonight, I don't think I could get it up for something like what I had with Kimmy. You are the only woman I ever want to be with."

"Good." I stand on tiptoe, pressing a kiss to his chin. "Because I'll be hanging on to you."

Gabe hugs me until I grunt. "Hang on tight."

"I plan to." I seal the words with a kiss, but I don't really think I'll have to cling too tightly. Even after all we've been through, I'm still stupid enough to think the worst is over, a belief that would soon be proved very, very wrong.

CHAPTER
Eleven

Gabe

"I love you more than words can wield the matter,
Dearer than eyesight, space and liberty."
-Shakespeare

The next time we make love is slow and sweet. I come into Caitlin with my heart so full it feels like it's about to burst, and by the time we shatter—within seconds of each other, our cries muffled by a kiss—I am even more hers than I was before.

I am a part of her, and she is a part of me, and I am home.

After, I'm more exhausted than I can remember being since the surgery, but I stay awake as long as I can. I lie with my eyes open in the dark, staring at the flat white paint of the hotel ceiling, memorizing the miracle that is Caitlin asleep on my chest, before I finally drift off around two in the morning.

When the pounding on the door comes three hours later, it feels like I've only been out for a few minutes. Caitlin is up and out of bed, tugging on my gray tee shirt, and hurrying across the room before I've managed to lift my head from the pillow. She cracks the door, sending a shaft of light piercing through the gloom to fall across the foot of the bed.

I hear an urgent mumble from outside, then Caitlin whispering something soft and reassuring, and then a voice that sounds like Danny's saying—

"No, now, Caitlin. I'm fucking worried. I need to go."

I swing out of bed, running a hand down my sleep-slack face as I move to join Caitlin at the door, but she shuts it just before I reach her side, plunging the suite back into semi-darkness.

"What's wrong?" I draw her into my arms, relishing the fresh-from-bed warmth of her body.

"Danny just got off the phone with his girlfriend in Hawaii," she says, resting her cheek on my chest with a sigh. "Her parents are getting a divorce, and she's really upset. He's saying he wants to fly back right now, but there's no way I can let him fly alone, not when there's no one there to meet him at the airport."

"Isn't it the middle of the night there?" I ask, trying to calculate the time difference with my brain still only semi-functional.

"Yes," Caitlin says, yawning. "That's part of why Danny's so upset. Sam's never called him so late. Or early...whatever time it is." She hugs me tight before pressing a kiss to the center of my bare chest. "I'm going to put on some shorts and see if I can settle him down before he wakes Sherry, and the rest of the kids. Go back to sleep."

"No, I'll come help," I say, running my hands up her hips, underneath my tee shirt to circle her waist. "But I'll need to reclaim my shirt first."

She laughs. "No way. It's soft and comfortable, and it smells like you."

I smile and pull her in for a kiss, touched that she loves the smell of me as much as I love the smell of her. She is my favorite smell. If I could smell nothing but Caitlin scent for the rest of my life, I would consider myself a lucky man.

"Besides, I think I should handle this

alone," she continues, mumbling the words against my lips before she pulls away from the kiss. "At least at first. Danny likes you a lot, but he isn't comfortable with having feelings, let alone having feelings around someone he hasn't seen in a while."

I nod and reluctantly let her slip from my arms. "All right. But come get me when you need me. I'll help any way I can."

"Thanks," she squeezes my hand. "Be back soon."

I return to bed, certain I won't be able to fall back asleep in a lonely room with no Caitlin in it, but I do. I sleep and dream of the morning I woke up from the surgery, when the sun was sifting through the filmy curtains of my hospital room, painting the world in miracle colors, but for some reason all I could feel was fear, sadness, and the overwhelming certainty that something so much more important than a chunk of my brain had been lost.

When I wake, my throat is tight and my jaw clenched so hard the centers of my teeth feel bruised. I shift my head, glancing at the clock, shocked to find it's already fifteen after eight.

That means that Bea, my former nurse, will be up walking her dog before she leaves for her nine o'clock shift at the hospital. If I call her now, I might catch her before she gets in the car. I reach for my phone on the bedside table and scroll through my contacts as I prop up against the pillows.

Bea gave me her number the day I woke up from the surgery. She'd spent the afternoon talking me down from bouts of panic and rage that frightened my parents and the other nurses, and seemed to understand how devastated I was in a way no one else could. At the end of her shift, she'd pressed her number into my hand and promised that she would always pick up the phone, no matter what time I needed to call.

I never used the number—knowing Bea would be back at nine almost every morning was enough to help me hold it together—but I have to use it now. I need answers, and Bea is the only person at the hospital that I trust to tell me the unvarnished truth.

I tap her number and put the phone to my ear, heart racing.

She picks up before the second ring and answers with a smile in her voice. "Mr. Gabriel! So nice to see your name this morning. How are you doing, sweet pea?"

"Much better, thank you, Bea," I say, realizing it's the truth. For the first time since the surgery, I feel nothing but hope for the future…assuming Caitlin and I can put the past to rest. "But I was hoping we could talk."

"Of course," she says, the words followed by the sound of a door closing. "Biscuit and I are just back from our walk. I can chat while I feed him, and get my lunch together."

"Thanks," I say, nervous now that I actually have her on the line. There's a chance that this conversation will prove I was an asshole who abandoned Caitlin without a second thought, but I have to know the truth.

"Don't be shy," Bea says, when I'm silent a beat too long. "Never knew you to be shy. Cranky as hell in the morning, and damned fussy about your eggs, but never shy."

I smile. "I'm not a morning person."

She snorts. "That's putting it mildly."

"But I'm in a good mood this morning. Just looking for some answers, and I thought you might be able to help."

"Assuming I can, I'm happy to," she says. "As long as you're not looking for confidential information on another patient, or wanting to know my dress size."

"No, nothing like that." I stand to pace the carpet beside the bed, too anxious to sit still. "I was wondering about when I first came to the clinic, about what kind of…head space I was in."

Bea clears her throat. "Head space?"

I pace a little faster. "You know, did I seem upbeat and optimistic about the procedure or was I—"

"Hell no," Bea interrupts. "Pardon my French, sweet pea, but upbeat and optimistic are the last words I'd use to describe you."

My lips twist. I'm grateful Bea is as frank as I remember. "What words would you use? I'd be grateful to hear them. And don't bother treading softly. I'm hunting hard truth this morning."

Bea sighs. "Well...I can't say I've ever met another pre-op like you, Gabe. Anxiety and depression are pretty common in patients getting ready to roll the dice with a surgery that has a better than average chance of ending badly, but you were...something else."

"Something like..." I prod.

"The day you were rolled in, it was like a dark cloud took up residence in my wing," Bea says, her Midwestern twang getting stronger the way it always did when she got riled up about something. "I swear, even the fluorescent lights seemed dimmer in your room."

"But I signed the consent forms for the surgery," I say. "I saw my signature the day I was released."

"You did. No one was holding a gun to your head, but you wouldn't have known it from the way you acted the day your dad brought you to check in."

"So I wasn't happy to be there?" I try to keep the relief from my tone, not wanting to bias Bea's account.

"No, you weren't happy. You were..." She's quiet for a moment, before continuing in a soft, sad voice. "Haunted is the word that comes to mind. It was like your spirit had already shriveled up and died, and you were just waiting for your body to follow suit. I honestly didn't expect you to make it through the surgery, honey. It's hard enough when people want to live, let alone when they've already given up."

I frown. "You don't think I wanted to live?"

"Sure didn't seem like it," she says. "You did ask me for the hard truth. Let me know if you want me to start sugar coating."

"No, I don't want sugar coating, I just..." I shake my head. Surely I would have wanted to live. I knew Caitlin was still out there somewhere, waiting for me...didn't I?

"Did I ever mention a woman to you, Bea?" I ask. "A girlfriend who was waiting on me back home, someone I cared about?"

"Not that I can remember," she says, making my stomach knot before she adds, "But you did call out a girl's name in your sleep that day before the surgery. Yelled it real loud a few times. I think it was...Kathy...Katy? Something like that?"

My bones melt with relief. "Caitlin?"

"Could have been. I've never been the best with names," she says, grunting softly. "There you go, Biscuit. You be a good boy today, and don't poop on my new rug again. This dog still isn't going on the puppy pad, Gabriel. Can you believe that? I'm beginning to think you're right, and I should have gotten a cat, instead."

"Don't listen to me, I was never allowed to have a pet, not even a fish," I say, still distracted, wondering why I was in such a hopeless place. Was it because I assumed the surgery wouldn't go well, or something more? And I still don't know how my parents convinced me to have the surgery without at least calling Caitlin first.

They must have had ammunition of some kind. Something serious enough to make me play along, no matter how much I objected to their plans.

"Well, I think that's a shame," Bea says. "Every kid should have a pet. I had a collie when I was growing up, sweetest thing in the world, treated me like one of her puppies."

"My parents aren't fans of things that drool and smell," I say with a grim smile. "Not human babies, let alone furry ones."

Bea makes a disapproving sound. "Well, just between you and me, I'm not the biggest fan of your parents. A little too chilly for my taste. I know you rich people like to keep your feelings to yourselves, but…"

I laugh. "Not me. Not anymore."

She coos, and I know she'd be pinching my cheek if we were in the same room. "Aw, Gabriel. You're in love. Good for you, honey. You enjoy it and don't look back. Those dark cloud days are behind you. It's going to be clear sailing from here on out, I can just feel it."

"I hope so, Bea." I thank her and wish her a wonderful rest of her summer before hanging up and reaching for my shorts from the day before. I pull them on, stuff a room key into my back pocket, and pad barefoot down the hall to the two-bedroom suite at the end of the hall, where Sherry and the kids are staying, past ready to see Caitlin again.

Even a few hours apart feels like too much.

CHAPTER
Twelve

Gabe

I'm about to knock on the door when it opens from the inside, revealing a sleepy looking Sherry in bright orange pajamas that clash with her wild red curls.

"Oh, hey," she says, laughing. "What's up? I'm going down for coffee and cinnamon buns. You want anything?"

"Coffee would be great," I say. "Do you need help carrying everything?"

"No, I can get it," she says, waving a hand as she eases past me and I reach out to hold the door open. "And Caitlin would probably appreciate your help at drama central. She and Danny are out on the balcony talking again, and Isaac has called five times this morning. I don't think Caitlin's answering, but I can tell it's stressing her out."

Sherry turns to go, but spins back. "Oh, and the other boys are still asleep, but Emmie was making noises, so you might want to keep an ear out. I'm not sure Caitlin and Danny will be able to hear her out on the balcony. The traffic noise from the street is pretty bad."

I smile. "Got it."

I step into the suite, a larger version of the room I checked into last night, with the same kitchenette area with a stove and refrigerator inside the door to the right. But instead of the bed straight ahead, there is a sitting room with a flat screen TV, and a sliding glass door leading onto a balcony. The curtains are closed, and I can't see Caitlin and Danny outside, but I take Sherry's word for it and head toward the sliding glass door.

Off the sitting room, there are two doors on either side, leading to the bedrooms. The one on the left is closed up tight, but the door on the right is ajar, and as I pass through the sitting room, I hear Emmie singing to herself. I can't understand the words to the song, but the tune makes me smile.

I peek inside to find Emmie in the middle of one of the two queen beds, surrounded by stuffed animals, making a koala bear and a giraffe dance across the sheets. She looks up, grinning when she sees me at the door.

"Hi, Gabe," she says. "Want to play animals?"

"How do you play animals?" I ask, moving into the room, which smells of Caitlin's shampoo and lavender and other scents that make it clear this is a girly space.

"You take one, and I take one," Emmie says, holding out the giraffe. "And then we pretend."

I settle on the edge of the bed and take the giraffe. "What should we pretend?"

"Koko on a scary rollercoaster," Emmie says, holding up the koala. "And Raff wants her to stop because he's afraid she's going to get hurt."

Without holding for more questions, Emmie mimes strapping Koko into a rollercoaster and proceeds to exclaim how excited she is to ride in a high, squeaky voice I can only assume is the koala's. Following her lead, I give Raff, the Giraffe, a high-pitched voice, and beg Koko to get off the rollercoaster before it's too late.

Koko proves immune to reason, and Raff is forced to resort to bribes and then threats, but Koko is determined to stay on the scary rollercoaster, even though the car is getting ready to jump over a pit of hot lava. Raff is in the midst of a fit of hysterics, and Koko is giggling her head off, when laughter comes from the entrance to the bedroom.

"This may be the best game of scary rollercoaster animals I've ever seen." I turn to find Caitlin leaning against the doorframe, smiling that loving smile that makes her look lit up from the inside. Even with dark circles under her eyes, she is still the most beautiful thing I've ever seen.

"Go away, Caitlin," Emmie says, reaching out and fisting her hand in my shorts. "We're playing now. You and Gabe can play later."

"Well, thanks, Emmie," Caitlin says, laughing. "Then, I guess I'll make myself scarce. Just wanted you to know that Sherry is back with cinnamon rolls."

"We aren't hungry yet, thank you." Emmie doesn't release her grip, clearly intending to hold me prisoner, a fact that is ridiculously satisfying.

"We'll play a little more," I say, smiling at Caitlin. "As long as you don't need me."

Caitlin shakes her head. "No, I'm fine. Danny and I both talked to Sam on the phone again, and it seemed to calm her down. She's going to sleep, and Danny's going to call her later this afternoon."

"What about the other calls?" I ask, not wanting to mention Isaac's name.

Caitlin sighs and lifts a weary shoulder. "They keep coming, I keep not answering. Hopefully they'll stop soon."

"I made a call this morning, too," I say. "To the clinic in Michigan where I had my surgery. I'll tell you all about it over coffee in a few."

Caitlin's eyebrows drift up, but before she can speak, Emmie tugs on my shorts and says—

"Come on, Gabe. Let's play."

So we do, for another fifteen minutes, that turns into twenty when Koko is seriously injured right as I tell Emmie that Raff needs to take a break to eat breakfast. I finally convince Emmie to join me in the kitchen by agreeing that Koko and Raff can sit next to her on her stool at the counter. I carry Emmie and the animals into the other room and get them settled with a cinnamon roll, before turning to accept a coffee from Caitlin.

"Thank you," I say before taking a grateful sip of the barely warm liquid.

Caitlin chuckles. "No one should have to play animals before coffee. It's probably a form of torture in some parts of the world."

I smile. "I had fun. Koko has a lot of personality."

"Tell me about it," Caitlin says, ruffling Emmie's blond curls as the little girl digs into her cinnamon roll. "Once Koko, Raff, and Pooty started talking, we couldn't get this one to stop."

"Pooty?" I lift an eyebrow.

"You haven't met Pooty?" Caitlin asks with a wicked grin. "Oh, but you will. Pooty is even louder than Koko. I'm sure you two will have a great time together."

"I can go get him," Emmie says, moving to slide off her stool before Caitlin stops her with a hand on her knee.

"Finish your breakfast first, okay? I need to talk to Gabe for a few minutes."

Emmie frowns and holds up one icing-coated finger. "One minute."

"Maybe more than one, but we'll be done by the time you finish your cinnamon roll, I promise." Caitlin takes my hand and leads me toward the balcony, past where the three boys are camped out on the couch watching TV while they eat, but a knock at the door stops her halfway across the room.

"Who could that be?" Caitlin asks, turning back to Sherry, who's still in the kitchen. "You expecting someone?"

Sherry shakes her head. "No, I didn't tell anyone where we were staying."

Caitlin's lips part, but before she can speak the knock comes again, more urgent this time. I step in front of her, instinctively wanting to protect her from whatever trouble might be at the door.

"Let me answer it." I cross the carpet to open the door before Caitlin can protest, peering through the peephole to find a man in wrinkled khaki pants and a white polo shirt that's a little tight across his rounded stomach.

I open the door a few inches. "Can I help you?"

"Good morning, is this Caitlin Cooney's room?" the man asks with a benign smile. He looks harmless, but so did Ned Pitt, and I'm not about to let him at Caitlin until I know what he wants.

"Do you mind telling me who's asking?" I say. "And why?"

The man pulls a manila envelope from behind his back. "I have a delivery. But I need to make sure it goes directly into Miss Cooney's hands."

"It's okay, Gabe," Caitlin says from behind me. I feel her cool fingers on my bare stomach and shift to the side, opening the door wide enough for her to stand beside me.

"What's the delivery?"

The man holds out the envelope, backing a step away the moment Caitlin has it in hand. "You've been served ma'am," he says with another efficient smile.

"What?" Caitlin's eyes go wide. "But I can't—"

"Have a good day." He turns, moving away down the hall, making a speedy getaway now that he's dropped a bomb in the middle of our morning.

Caitlin cusses softly and smacks the envelope with one hand before ripping into the top with shaking fingers.

"Your sister already?" I ask, unable to think of anyone else who would be filing a legal suit against Caitlin.

Caitlin pulls out the paperwork, paling as she scans the pages. "She's suing for custody, and she's managed to get an expedited motion to get us into court for an initial hearing before we fly back." She squeezes her eyes shut, and leans back against the doorframe. "She's got a court date, and I don't even have a lawyer."

"I'll make some calls right now," I say. "I know a couple of people in Charleston that my father doesn't care for, but who are supposed to be good. We'll see if one of them will take the case. That way we can be sure they won't carry the story back to my dad."

Caitlin sighs, and her eyes slide slowly open, as if it's an effort to move even those small muscles. "He's going to find out sooner or later."

"Let's try to make it later, at least until I know how they convinced me to go to Michigan without calling to tell you goodbye." I fill her in on my conversation with Bea, and watch her tired eyes grow troubled.

"They had something on you," Caitlin says, echoing my thoughts. "Something big."

"And I need to find out what before they try to use it again," I say. "Assuming it's the kind of blackmail that retains its effectiveness post brain-tumor."

Caitlin sighs again, a longer, heavier sound this time. "Can't anything ever be simple?"

I smile. "Yes. This morning will be. Go back to my room, and take a nap. I'll take care of the lawyer, and start trying to dig up dirt on your sister."

Caitlin shakes her head. "I need to run over to the department store and buy a hat. Or a scarf and glasses, something to wear to the funeral. Or maybe I shouldn't go, after all."

"I'll take care of the hat, too," I say, taking her by the shoulders and guiding her back down the hall. "You shouldn't let my parents keep you from your father's funeral if you want to go, and you shouldn't start a day like today exhausted or every bad thing will seem worse."

She smiles tiredly at me over my shoulder. "Are you sure this isn't an excuse to take me back to bed?"

"Not this time," I say. "But I will be reclaiming my shirt, so you'll have to sleep naked."

She lifts a brow. "Are you going to be able to resist if you see me naked?"

"No," I confess as I open the door and urge her inside. "That's why you're going in, and handing the shirt back through a crack in the door."

She laughs, but the sound fades quickly, and when she turns back to me, she looks scared. "Aoife can't take Emmie away, can she? I mean, surely even she can see that Emmie is better off staying with the only family she's ever known, right? Maybe if I try to talk to her again today, and keep my temper in check…"

I shrug. "It doesn't matter. If Aoife sees that what she's doing is selfish, great. If not, I'll hire the best lawyer money can buy, and you'll crush her in court. And I'll start looking into her story this morning, see if I can find anything we can use to blackmail her into going away. No matter what we have to do, we'll take care of it. Emmie is staying with you. Where she belongs."

Caitlin looks comforted, but I'm glad when she hides behind the door and hands out my shirt, and I'm spared looking into her eyes. I want her to get her rest, but I'm not sure everything is going to be okay. The more I think about what Bea said, the more I worry that whatever my parents had against me is something no amount of muscle or money or quick thinking it going to be able to make go away.

CHAPTER
Thirteen

Caitlin

"Earth's crammed with heaven...
But only he who sees takes off his shoes."
-Elizabeth Barrett Browning

Y ou never forget your first funeral.

Mine was for Great Uncle Tom, who had a heart attack in his peach orchard while checking to see how his new stinkbug poison was performing. He was dead almost two days before Great Aunt Maryanne finally went looking for him. She found him curled up next to his John Deere, bloated in the mid-summer heat, and attracting flies.

The body was in terrible shape, but Maryanne insisted on an open casket. I heard the funeral home director tried to talk her out of it, but Maryanne was a stubborn cuss—the only reason she was able to stay married to a cranky bastard like Uncle Tom for fifty-eight years. She insisted on an open casket, and on Tom being squeezed into the good Sunday suit he hadn't worn since the day a decade previous when he'd told Maryanne he was too old to waste a perfectly good Sunday bruising his ass on a church pew.

The funeral was held in a tiny country church out a long dirt road, somewhere close to Uncle Tom and Aunt Mary's farm, though I can't remember seeing it before, or since. But I remember stepping through the door, into the stifling heat of a one-room wood plank building with no air conditioning.

I remember holding Aoife's hand so tight the sweat building between our palms dripped onto the dusty floor, and the gray, lumpish face of Uncle Tom peeking up above the top of the casket, looking like something out of a horror movie. I remember the way his chin seemed to be sliding back into his neck, and how terrified I was that his mouth was going to open up and something was going to come flying out. Daddy had said something to Mama in the car about flies laying eggs in dead bodies. I was in the backseat with all the

LILI VALENTE

windows rolled down, and wasn't meant to hear, but I did.

I had nightmares for weeks after Uncle Tom's funeral. I'd wake up shaking and sweating, feeling like something horrible was crawling up my throat and roll over and hug Aoife so tight she'd wake up groaning. But she never yelled at me. She would simply hug me, sweep my damp hair from my forehead, and tell me it was only a dream until I relaxed enough to go back to sleep.

Once upon a time, Aoife was my rock. I loved her like a mother, a sister, and a best friend all wrapped up together, but that was a long time ago.

Right now, watching her settle into a pew at the front of the church next to Veronica, Veronica's two daughters, and all the Cooney cousins and second cousins, all I feel is angry and afraid. I wish she'd stayed in Florida. I wish I'd never been forced to see her face again, or realize I mean so little to the woman I once considered the most beautiful, perfect, necessary person in the world.

Aoife is here for Emmie, not to mend fences with me. The fact that I rearranged my entire life and have worked, suffered, and sacrificed to pick up the slack when Aoife left means nothing to her. *I* mean nothing to her.

I am just another person who has outlived my usefulness, and must now be cast aside. It's the way Aoife works. She's a lot like Dad that way, but this time I refuse to make discarding people easy for her. She's going to look this ugly thing she's doing in the face, and see how much damage she's preparing to inflict.

I stay at the back of the church during the service, the navy straw hat Gabe bought to match my navy sheath pinned into my upswept hair, my veil pulled over my face, and my eyes on the hands folded in my lap. I haven't seen any sign of the Alexanders— Gabe said his dad was at work and his mom was consulting for new interior design clients at the country club—but I figure it's better to be safe than sorry. I keep a low profile, and when the service is over and Chuck's body is being carried out, I circle around the other side of the church, intercepting Aoife before she can start for the parking lot, where two limos are waiting to take family members on to the graveside service.

"Can I talk to you?" I ask softly, stepping out from between the pews to block her path.

She sniffs and wipes tears from beneath her eyes. "I don't think we should. My lawyer says I shouldn't speak to you until everything is settled." She looks almost as tired as I feel, and for the first time I wonder if maybe this isn't as easy for her as I'd assumed.

Maybe, deep down, she knows trying to take Emmie away is wrong. Maybe if I can get her alone, and say the right things, this can all go away.

"Please, Aoife," I beg, ignoring the hard look Veronica shoots my way as she moves up the aisle to hover near my sister's elbow. "We're sisters. Let's talk this out, okay? I don't want to fight with you."

"Then you need to give the girl her baby back," Veronica says, in a hard voice I haven't heard from her before. "She's Emmie's mama. That's her kid, Caitlin, not yours."

I'm tempted to snap that Emmie isn't a possession, but if anyone is going to lay claim to my niece, it's me. I'm the one who has loved her, paid for her, and cared about her for nearly four years, not Aoife. But that would be a waste of breath. Veronica's opinion doesn't matter, and picking a fight in church isn't part of my agenda.

Brawling at a funeral would be too typically Cooney, and I've always tried to rise above my family's reputation, not lie down and wallow in it.

"Please," I ask again, holding my sister's tired eyes. "Just give me two minutes in private. That's all I'm asking."

I see Aoife wavering, but before she speaks, Veronica loops her arm through my sister's and proceeds to voice her full twelve cents on the matter.

"This girl has been to hell and back, and turned her life around. Do you know how hard that is?" She props a fist on her full hips, blocking the path of the two older men trying to move around her, making sure we have an audience. "You should be proud of her, and doing whatever you can to support her, not trying to tear her down and take her baby away."

I literally have to bite my tongue to hold back my response to that. I bite it hard enough to break the skin and send the bitter, salty taste of blood rushing through my mouth.

"It's okay, V. But thank you, I appreciate it," Aoife says, already more cozy with our father's ex-girlfriend in two days, than I am after years of acquaintance.

But Aoife has always been good at making allies when she needs them. Back in seventh grade, she enlisted her own team of bodyguards from the girls' track team, all with nothing more than a sob story about another group of girls threatening to beat her up after school, a delicate smile, and a few free manicures during lunch.

"We can talk," Aoife says, turning back to me. "But I only have a few minutes. I'm going with Veronica in her limo."

"You can ride with us, too, Caitlin," Veronica says, moving up the aisle, allowing the people she's trapped to move past her on the other side. "I'm not the kind to push someone out of the family because they're doing something I don't like. Love the sinner, hate the sin, that's my belief."

Somehow, through sheer force of will, I manage not to roll my eyes until she's turned her back, but then I roll them hard enough to send a flash of pain shooting through my eyelids.

"I know, but she means well," Aoife says, surprising me as we move between the pews, off to the right side of the church. "She's a strong woman. I'm glad Dad had someone like her in his life at the end. It sounds like they got along a lot better than Mom and Dad ever did."

"Have you heard from Mom?" I ask as we reach the far aisle and stand beneath the stained glass windows illustrating the Stations of the Cross. The sun streaming through the colored glass casts Aoife's pale face in a golden light, making her look even more angelic—and more like Mom—than usual.

I used to think their physical similarities were the reason she and Mom were always close, but now I suspect it's their mutual love of revising history that allowed them to maintain a relationship long after I cut Mom out of my life. I don't like lies to begin with, but hearing miserable situations from my childhood filtered through my mother's rose-colored glasses was especially torturous. Those months I spent with a horrible foster family weren't "a good growing experience," and the time she dropped me off at school on a Sunday and left me there all day wasn't a "funny story." Not any funnier than the other traumatizing events of my childhood.

Aoife shakes her head. "Not for about a year. She came to visit me right after Mitch and I got the house, but then she brought home a six-pack of beer. Mitch flipped out and made her leave. He had my cell phone number changed after, so she hasn't been able to call, and I promised Mitch I wouldn't call her. He's really committed to helping me stay sober, so…"

"That's good," I say, though I'm thinking that the guy sounds like a control freak. But maybe that's what Aoife needs to stay clean. If so, I'm glad she found someone who meets her needs, I just don't want Emmie growing up in that kind of environment. "I'm glad you're so much better. You know that, right?"

Her lips curve in a sad smile. "You just don't think I can keep it up? Is that what you're worried about? I've been clean for almost eighteen months, Caitlin. It's going to stick this time. I promise."

"That's not what I'm worried about," I say. "I'm worried about Emmie. That's all this is. She had a lot of developmental problems for the first few years after she was born, but she's been doing so much better. I don't want her to backslide, and I think being taken away from the only family she's ever known would be really devastating for her."

"But I'm her mother, Caitlin," Aoife says, pleading with her eyes for me to understand. "I know I screwed up, but that doesn't mean I have to lose my daughter forever, does it? I mean…I'm different now, and I just want another chance. I'm tired of paying for all those old mistakes."

"I get it, Aoife, I really do, but life doesn't work that way," I say, throat tight with emotion. "You can't just wave a magic wand and erase the things you don't like about your past. Your actions affected people in dramatic ways, ways that have lasting results."

"Only if people insist on continuing to punish me for a crime I've already paid for." Aoife crosses her arms protectively over her stomach. "I've already lost almost four years of Emmie's life. I don't want to lose any more."

"You don't have to." I don't want to compromise with Aoife, but it might be the only way to get out of here without going to court. "We could split custody. I could have Emmie during the school year, and she could come stay with you every summer and Christmas, or something like that. We could make it work with your schedule."

Aoife's brows draw together and she blinks at me like I've said something nonsensical. "I'm not going to split custody. Mitch doesn't want that. He wants to adopt Emmie, and for all of us to be a family. We just want to be normal, Caitlin."

"And I wanted to stay in high school, and get a scholarship to college," I say, beginning to lose my temper. "And Emmie wanted to be born without developmental delays caused by her mom using drugs while she was pregnant."

Aoife's mouth drops open, but I push on before she can speak.

"But it didn't work out that way. We don't always get what we want, Aoife," I say, forcing a gentler note into my tone. "But if we work together, we can make choices that are the best for your daughter. It might not be ideal for you or me, but it will be what's best for Emmie."

"My daughter needs her mother," Aoife says, but I hear the doubt crimping the edges of the words.

"Your daughter needs the same thing she's always needed, someone to love her and take care of her and make her feel safe, and I have done a damned good job of that," I say, driving my argument home and praying I can finish getting through to my sister. "Taking her away from a loving family—a family we would have killed for when we were kids—is pure selfishness, plain and simple."

"Then I guess I'm a selfish bitch," she says, tears streaming down her flushed cheeks. "Because I'm not dropping the suit. I want to be happy, and I'm not letting you take that away from me."

I start to tell her that I don't give a shit about her happiness one way or another, but she pushes past me, throwing her parting shot over her shoulder.

"I have to go bury my father now."

Her father. As if I didn't love him and hate him and live in the long shadow he cast every bit as much as she did. As if I didn't stay in town and take care of his house and his laundry and his kids and try to make sure he ate a decent meal now and then for years after she left me alone.

The injustice of that stupid "my" is the final straw. I decide to skip the graveside, family-only service and head back to my real family—Gabe, Sherry, and the kids. I slip through the small crowd of mourners still gathered in front of the church and start swiftly toward the parking lot. I don't intend to cast a single glance toward the limos parked at the curb, or any of the people waiting to get in them, but as I lift my purse to dig for my keys, I catch sight of an elegant figure in a dark gray suit in my peripheral vision.

Even before I turn my head, my pulse is already speeding.

I know that silhouette. I've only met Gabe's father a handful of times, but he and Gabe are the same height, with the same broad shoulders, and long legs, and the same way of tilting their head when they're listening to something they're really interested in hearing.

Right now, Aaron Alexander is standing

next to the family limo, head cocked as he listens to something my sister is saying. I'm too far away to catch any of Aoife's words, but when she swipes tears from her cheeks and motions back over her shoulder toward the church, I have a pretty good idea who she's talking about.

"Shit," I curse. So much for lying low until we find out what Gabe's parents used to blackmail him last summer.

With one last look at the impeccably well-dressed man questioning my sister, I turn and start toward the car. But I force myself to walk, not run. Chuck always said that you should never run from danger. Running lets the bad guys know you're afraid, and attracts their attention. Better to slip away slow and steady, and hope something more vulnerable-looking than you catches their eye. And so I maintain a calm, even gait before slipping into the van and easing slowly out of the parking lot unobserved.

Maybe Chuck did teach me one or two things of value, after all.

But only one or two and that might not be enough to hold my family together through whatever the Alexanders have up their sleeves.

CHAPTER
Fourteen

Caitlin

"Life loves to be taken by the lapel and told,
'I'm with you kid. Let's go.'"
-Elizabeth Barrett Browning

I arrive back at the hotel an hour and a half before I promised to find Sherry and the kids already out at the pool. I park the van, pull off my hat, and let my hair out of the knot that's pinching the back of my head, before slamming out the door and crossing to the fence.

The moment Sherry sees my face, she knows something's wrong. "Oh God." She stands, tugging the bottom of her pink and white polka-dot one piece down as she tosses her *Wired* magazine onto her lounge chair. "Aoife was horrible."

"Aoife was horrible, and then Gabe's dad showed up," I say, hurrying on when Sherry's eyes go wide. "He didn't see me, but I'm pretty sure Aoife is going to tell him we're in town. They were talking when I left."

"What are you going to do?" she whispers, casting a glance over her shoulder to make sure none of the kids are close enough to hear. "I mean, I'd like to think Mr. Alexander is harmless, but he did blackmail his son into having surgery, then fake Gabe's funeral. I'm not sure he's dealing with a full deck."

I nod, pressing my lips tight together. "I'm going to go talk to Gabe. We may move to another hotel. Somewhere in Charleston maybe, where it will be harder to find us. I want to know the kids are safe."

Sherry crosses her arms, looking chilled despite the hot summer day. "I wish we could go back to Maui. Giffney is giving me the creeps. I never realized how messed up this town was until I left. It's like…the place where dreams go to die."

"You can go home if you want to," I say, hating that I've dragged my best friend into this crazy situation. "I have to stay until the court date, but—"

"No way." Sherry shakes her head. "I'm not leaving until I'm sure you're going to have your happily ever after. Mr. Sexy is in the room, by the way. He was trying to dig up dirt on your sister, but your phone was blowing up. I think it was driving him a little nuts. I tried to turn it off, but it was still vibrating every time Isaac called."

I roll my eyes and let out a sound somewhere between a groan and a muffled scream.

"I know, when it rains, it pours." Sherry shoots me a sympathetic look. "It just wouldn't be your life if you didn't have to bury your father, while dealing with the return of the sister from hell, a custody battle, a boyfriend back from the grave, and an ex-boyfriend who's discovering his obsessive streak."

In spite of the nightmare morning, I have to smile. "I love you, you know that?"

Sherry grins. "And I love you, despite the fact that you appear to have been born under the unluckiest star ever."

"I don't know. I'm still feeling pretty lucky right now." I turn to look toward Gabe's room to see him out on the balcony. I lift my hand and wave, but he stops me with an urgent motion of his arm.

"You need to come look at this," he calls out, holding up his phone.

I let my arm drop with a sigh. "I'll be back to spring you in a few," I tell Sherry.

"Don't rush," she says. "We just got out here a few minutes ago. The kids are playing great, and my sister can't get free until dinner tonight so I don't have anywhere to be."

"Thanks." I squeeze her hand through the gate and hurry up to the room.

I'm not looking forward to telling Gabe about his dad—or learning whatever it is that has him upset—but I can't wait to be in his arms. Every second away from him feels like a second I've wasted. I wish we could escape from the world and spend a week or two alone together, making love, lying in the sun, and doing nothing worthwhile except finishing the job of falling for each other harder the second time than we fell the first.

When I turn the corner on our floor, Gabe is standing in the doorway to his room, dressed in dark blue jeans and a pale blue tee shirt he picked up this morning while he was buying my hat. The shirt molds to his impressive new muscles and emphasizes the ice blue of his eyes. I've always thought Gabe's eyes would be equally at home in the face of an Alaskan hunting dog, or some kind of supernatural predator, but I can't say I've ever seen them look quite as menacing as they do right now.

"What happened?" I ask, knowing immediately that he has to go first.

"I need you to see something." He moves back, holding the door open wide enough for me to move past him into the room.

Inside, the bed is still disheveled and the desk is littered with pieces of hotel stationary with notes written on them in Gabe's elegant handwriting. Danny once said that Gabe makes eye-contact like a psychopath—I'd told my brother that's the kind of eye contact I like—but Gabe's handwriting looks like it flowed from the pen of an eighteenth century schoolteacher. It's gorgeous and makes me think of heartfelt letters, poems, and things lovers sent each other in another age.

It's one of the little things that make Gabe Gabe, things I want to unearth like buried treasure, piece by piece. I want to focus on rediscovering all the things I love about him as we move into the future together, but with every passing moment, escaping the past feels more impossible.

"I didn't mean to invade your privacy." Gabe plucks my phone from where it's resting on top of the notes. "But your phone was ringing every ten to fifteen minutes, and I wanted to know if it was the same person. I figured if it was, they either had a legitimate emergency, or might be a threat we'd want to be aware of."

I nod, pressing my lips together. "It was Isaac, right? Sherry said he was taking a walk on the stalker side."

"He's something worse than a stalker," Gabe says, the ominous note in his voice making the hairs on my arms stand on end. "This is his picture, I assume."

He holds up the phone. Isaac's contact information is pulled up on the screen, and the picture of Isaac on the afternoon of his graduation from the police academy grins back at me from the corner.

"That's him." My brow furrows as I glance back up at Gabe. Before I can ask him why he wanted to know, he places my phone back on the desk and pulls his from his back pocket.

"When I saw his picture, I thought he looked familiar," Gabe says, scrolling through something on his screen. "I thought it was because you said I'd met him last summer, but then I remembered where I'd seen his face."

He holds up the phone. "My private nurse after the surgery, Olia, was from Sweden, but she had a thing for pizza. Wood-fired pizza was her favorite."

I take the phone from him, holding it at a different angle to reduce the glare from the window.

"We went to the same place every Wednesday afternoon," Gabe continues. "We weren't supposed to leave the house without one of my parents, but they have couples therapy on Wednesdays, and Olia was okay with breaking the rules in the name of a sausage pie with extra onions."

I bring the image closer to my face, trying to see what has Gabe so shaken up. It's a fairly benign-looking selfie, taken by a fresh-faced older blond woman with her hair pulled back in a ponytail. She's grinning as she leans in close to Gabe. His smile looks more like a grimace, but it's the sunken places beneath his eyes and the skeletal way his skin stretches across his cheeks that breaks my heart.

"You were so sick," I say, fighting to swallow past the lump in my throat.

"I was getting better then," he says, dismissively, obviously not interested in my pity. "Don't look at me. Look behind me. Over by the counter. He's not in focus, but you can tell it's him."

I shift my gaze, and feel like I've been kicked in the gut. My breath rushes out, but it doesn't rush back in. For a moment it feels like I've forgotten how to reason, how to add up two and two to make four. My brain insists this can't be real, but my gut knows it is.

It knows, and the horrible knowledge races through my veins like a thousand tiny glass shards.

I suck in a ragged breath. "When was this taken?"

"September," Gabe says in a voice that makes it clear he's already tracked the timeline and realized this was before I lost the baby, before Isaac flew to Maui to help his "friend," and ended up staying to be my lover.

"He knew," I whisper, fingers digging into Gabe's black phone case. "He had to know it was you. Even though you'd lost weight, I knew right away that—"

"Oh, he knew." Gabe takes the phone gently from my hand, tossing it onto the desk as if he can't stand to touch it. "The first time we went in, he looked at me like he'd seen a ghost. I explained about my memory loss and asked if I'd known him before, but he said that I looked like someone he used to know. After that, every time Olia and I went in, he stayed out of our way. I'd put him out of my mind, but now..."

"Oh my God." My knees give out and I sit

down hard on the thick, gray carpet. "He knew you were alive. He knew I was so devastated and that I was pregnant, and he still… He let me believe…."

Gabe sits down in front of me, resting his hands on my knees, but he doesn't say a word, as if he knows nothing he can say right now will help.

"He let me fuck him," I say, rage rushing in to banish the betrayal, shoving it aside with hot hands balled into fists. "He fucked me, and told me he loved me, and all along he knew that the person I really loved was still alive."

"I'm sure he would say he did it out of love for you," Gabe says, in that silky voice that he gets when he's really angry. With some people, rage makes them rough around the edges, but it makes Gabe smooth, calm, as cold as a frozen lake about to crack under your feet.

I bite my lip. "He did it because he knew there was no way he stood a chance if I knew the truth."

Gabe leans in, until our foreheads are nearly touching before he whispers, "I want to do horrible things to this man. I want to make him suffer for every minute he made you suffer, and for every second he kept you from me."

I shiver. My eyes slide closed and for a second I can't keep from imagining the way I'd make Isaac pay, the way I'd exact my vengeance if I had nothing to lose, and not a trace of morality. But that's not who I am. Isaac isn't innocent, but he isn't a monster, either, and I could never do to him the things I've done to my other marks, no matter how much a part of me might want to.

"I can't," I say softly, still not opening my eyes. "I hate him, but…I can't hurt him."

"Maybe I can," Gabe says.

I slit my lids, staring at his lips through my lashes, trying to tell from the set of his mouth if he's serious. His mouth keeps its secrets, but when I pull away to look into his eyes, I see the truth.

"You're not going to hurt Isaac."

He sighs. "No, I'm not. But we're not going to be able to play by the rules, Caitlin. Not if we want to be together. I listened to the messages Isaac left."

I chew the inside of my cheek, holding my breath as I wait for him to tell me the rest of the bad news.

"After the first three messages, demanding you call him, Isaac left a tearful message begging for your forgiveness. He swore he was only trying to protect you. He said you have to leave Giffney right away."

I frown. "How did he know I was here?"

"He said his mother told him last night," Gabe says, arching a brow. "She heard it from a girl who works at the pizza place."

"Kimmy's friend." I curse, driving a hand through my hair and fisting it on the top of my head. "I can't catch a break in this town."

"That's what Isaac seemed worried about." Gabe guides my hand from my hair before I can do myself damage, and pulls me into his lap. "He feels awful for letting you believe I was dead, but says he did it because my parents swore you'd end up in jail if you ever came back to South Carolina."

My gaze snaps to his face. "What?"

"Isaac promised them he'd keep you in Hawaii," Gabe says. "And they were nice enough to pay his plane fare in exchange. He confessed everything in message four."

The angry heat swirling in my chest cools a few degrees. I'm shocked that Isaac was in on this—Isaac, one of the few people in the world I would have trusted with my life—but there's a bigger threat in those words. "Your parents don't know about the things we did. Do they?"

Gabe shakes his head just once, back and

forth. "I don't know, but I don't want to stay to find out. I think we should leave."

I twine my arms around his shoulders, needing something to hold on to. "But I can't leave. I'm due in court at the end of the week. The earliest I can leave the state would be next week, and that's if—"

"I'm not talking about leaving the state," he says. "I'm talking about leaving the country."

CHAPTER
Fifteen

Caitlin

"Why, what is to live? Not to eat and drink and breathe,
—but to feel the life in you down all the fibres of being."
-Elizabeth Barrett Browning

I blink, but the look in his eyes leaves no doubt he's serious.

"I've been thinking about this since you left for the funeral," Gabe says. "I was dead set against the surgery, and was prepared to die. My parents had no leverage as far as I was concerned. Nothing, except how much I cared for you."

"So you think—"

"The only thing that could have gotten me on that plane was knowing that, if I didn't, something bad would happen to you," he says, echoing my thoughts. "And what could be worse than you ending up in jail for crimes *I* convinced you to commit?"

"Oh God," I say, throat clenching and a wave of sickness roiling through my belly. "But how did they find out? We were so careful. And our faces were covered and—"

"Like I said, I don't know," Gabe says. "I've done everything but slammed my head into the wall trying to remember, but I can't. Maybe I never will, since it happened on one of the last days before the surgery, but I've remembered enough to be ninety-nine percent certain my parents got to me through you, and I refuse to let them ruin your life."

My tongue slips out to dampen my suddenly bone dry lips, while my thoughts race. "What are we going to do?"

"I contacted my old fence in Charleston," Gabe says. "He knows a guy who is going to set us up with passports and birth certificates under different names. I've already taken pictures of the kids and sent them over. I told him I'd get our pictures to him this afternoon."

I shake my head hard enough to send my

hair flying around my face. "No, Gabe. I can't do that to them. A life spent running isn't any better than if they ended up in the system. I can't—"

"It will be a hell of a lot better than if they ended up in the system." Gabe stands, lifting me in his arms, carrying me across the room. "I've already booked a cottage on the coast of Croatia, a lovely country with a stable government, an excellent exchange rate, and no extradition policy for people accused of crimes on U.S. soil."

"What?" I let out a soft *oof* of surprise as he lays me on the bed.

He smiles. "We'll be staying in a beach town by the Adriatic Sea. It will be just like the Italian Riviera, only cheaper."

"Cheaper," I echo, mesmerized as he reaches for the bottom of his tee shirt and pulls it over his head. Even at a moment like this, the sight of his bare chest is enough to make my fingers itch with the need to touch him

"We check in on Wednesday." Gabe lies down beside me, his hand coming to rest at my waist, making my skin tingle beneath the scratchy fabric of my dress. "We'll have the cottage for the rest of the summer, long enough to decide whether we want to stay where we are and homeschool the boys, or move to the city, where they have an English-speaking school."

"You can't be for real." I stare deep into his eyes, seeing nothing but determination.

"Do I look like I'm not for real?" He lifts one brow as his fingers bunch the fabric of my dress, pulling my skirt higher on my thighs. "I have enough money to cover our expenses for years if we're relatively frugal. I've already transferred a sizeable amount into a Swiss bank account. We'll have access to the funds as soon as we land."

"But what about when the kids get older?" I ask, covering his hands with my own, the enormity of this conversation enough to make my head spin without Gabe undressing me at the same time. "We can't run away to a foreign country forever. What if the kids want to go to college in the states, or—"

"Then they go to college in the states." He brushes my hands away and finishes bunching my dress around my waist. "And they can come visit us on their breaks. We *can* run away forever, Caitlin. You and me." He leans in, kissing me with a tenderness that is every bit as arousing as the way he fists his hand in the top of my pantyhose. "We can go somewhere no one knows our names, and be a family."

My breath rushes out over his lips. "Gabe, I—"

"I've already got our story figured out," he interrupts, sitting up long enough to strip my pantyhose down my thighs and toss them to the floor before lying back down beside me. "We'll tell people that you were given custody of your brothers after your parents passed away, and that you and I are married, and Emmie is our daughter."

Tears spring to my eyes and my throat feels like it's about to close up, but I don't know if it's from gratitude or fear. I reach for Gabe, wrapping my arms around his neck and drawing him closer.

"Are you sure you want this?" I ask as he presses kisses to my throat and my pulse speeds faster. "Your parents don't want to ruin your life; they just want me to go away. Maybe, if I do, things can go back to the way they were. You can go back to school and have the life you wanted, and—"

"All I want is you." He pulls back to look me in the eyes, an intensity in his gaze that steals the rest of my words away. "You are the only thing I want, the only thing that makes my life worth living. You are everything to me."

I blink, sending tears streaming down my

cheeks. "You, too. To me."

Relief flickers in his eyes. "And that's all we need."

"But what about jobs?" I ask, still having a hard time wrapping my head around all this. "We'll eventually need jobs, and I don't even know what language they speak in Croatia."

"Croatian," he says, rubbing my tears into my skin with the pad of this thumb. "And I told you, I have enough money to hold us over for years. That's more than enough time to learn a new language."

"But what about visas and friends for the kids and—"

"We'll figure it all out," he says, bringing a finger to my lips. "I don't care what kind of work I do, or what language I speak. As long as we belong to each other, and I get to tell you I love you every day, I will be the happiest man in the world. You're my home, Caitlin, and I—"

I silence him with a kiss, too overcome to tell him how much everything he's said means to me. I have to show him. I have to show him with my body and soul that he is my home, too. He is my friend, my lover, and my saving grace. He is my partner, my other half, and one of the few people in the world I would fight to the death to protect.

He is the dream I didn't know I was wishing for until it came true, and one lifetime will never be enough to show him how lucky I feel to have been entrusted with his heart.

"I love you so much," I say between kisses, breath coming faster.

"Nothing can scare me, except thinking of another day without you in it."

I sigh into him and he inhales, breathing my breath. "You're pretty romantic, you know that?"

"I'll show you romantic." He kisses me hard enough to make my lips feel bruised, before he whispers, "Roll over onto your belly. I want to fuck you from behind."

I obey without a second of hesitation, rolling over and sweeping my hair to one side, shivering as Gabe draws my zipper down, curls his fingers into the front of my collar, and strips my dress from my body with one smooth movement, leaving me in nothing but my bra and panties. I reach back, intending to unhook my bra, needing to eliminate the barriers to being naked with the man I love, but Gabe brushes my hands away.

"No. This is my job," he says, kissing his way down my neck as he makes quick work of my bra and underwear.

A moment later he is on top of me,

blanketing me with his body, surrounding me so completely there is nothing but him—his smell, his taste, the feel of his strong arms sliding beneath me to cup my breasts, his erection nestled between the cheeks of my ass. I moan, arching back into the burning length of him, amazed that he can feel so hard and so soft at the same time. His need is rock solid as it presses against my tailbone, but his skin is petal soft, fever hot. The feel of that pulsing flesh so close to where I ache for him is enough to send a rush of liquid heat from my body.

"I love your cock," I whisper, moaning as he rocks forward, grinding against me, intensifying the throbbing between my legs. "I can't wait to get my tongue on you again. I want to taste every inch of you."

"Not today," he says, kissing his way across my shoulder as his fingers tease my nipples, making me cry out from the combined erotic friction of his touch, and my sensitive skin rubbing against the sheets. "Today, I'm going to pin you to this bed and fuck you until you know that you are mine, and I am yours, and nothing will ever come between us again."

"Yes." I reach back, digging my fingernails into the thick muscles of his ass, pulling him closer.

"God, Caitlin." He groans as I arch my back even farther, in what I hope is a clear invitation. "You drive me crazy." His teeth nip into my shoulder while one of his hands slides down to tease my clit in gentle circles.

My blood pressure spikes so fast my head spins. "Fuck me, Gabe," I beg as I wiggle my hips against him. "Don't make me wait. I need you."

"I need you, too," he says, fingers moving in firmer circles against my swollen nub, bringing me within seconds of tumbling over. "Let me get a condom."

"I'm on the pill," I say, hooking my feet around his ankles and holding him captive, certain I'll die if I'm deprived of the feel of his body for even a second. "I'm on the pill, it's okay. I want to feel your bare—"

My words end in a cry of satisfaction as he shifts his hips, finding my slick center with the blunt head of his cock and driving inside. With my legs together, it's a tighter fit than usual. Gabe has to force his way through the resistance, and for a moment it hurts, but then he is buried in my body, his hard length encased inside my heat, and it is pure bliss.

Bliss made all the sweeter because of that moment of pain.

It's like me and Gabe, I realize as he pulls

back and drives home again, making my entire body sing. The pain of losing him has made this second chance even more precious and beautiful. What we have is sacred, a bond forged by pain and pleasure, suffering and passion, and Gabe is right—nothing will tear us apart again. This is forever, for keeps, for the rest of our lives, no matter what the future holds.

"You're mine," I breathe, shoving back against him, wanting more of him, all of him.

"And you are mine," Gabe growls against my neck as he rides me harder, deeper, until every cell in my body is electrified with pleasure, and I'm squirming beneath him, so close my blood rockets through my veins.

His fingers are still busy between my legs and at my left breast, sending shockwaves of pleasure zipping from my head to my toes and back again, threatening to short-circuit my nerve endings. I'm not sure my body can handle the orgasm building to a fierce crescendo inside of me, but then Gabe shoves home one last time—coming so hard his cock jerks inside me—and my own release hits with enough force to take my breath away.

I explode like a firework painting the sky, like a bomb filled with flower petals showering the world with color, happiness, and hope. I come laughing and crying, clinging to Gabe's arm, and biting down on my bottom lip so hard it hurts, which for some reason makes me start laughing all over again.

"You okay?" Gabe kisses my cheek, his tongue slipping out to lap away one of my tears.

"Happy tears," I say, my voice trembling in the aftermath of one of the most intense orgasms of my life.

"Tasted like a happy tear." He bands his arms around my chest, hugging me tight. "I love the tattoo, by the way. It's stunning."

I smile. "We were going to get matching tattoos, remember?"

"I remember. Dandelion flowers, with the seeds blowing away, off in different directions, but from the same source." He kisses the place where my flower bends across my shoulder. "But I think I'll get something different once we're settled."

"Dandelions not good enough for you?" I turn my head and he shifts to rest his face on the pillow beside mine, though his body stays buried inside me, exactly where I want him to be.

"I was thinking about Shakespeare's 'Sonnet 116,' " he says, his eyelids droopy with pleasure. " 'Let me not to the marriage of true minds admit impediments. Love is not love, which alters when it alteration finds, or bends with the remover to remove. O no; it is an ever-fixed mark, that looks on tempests, and is never shaken.' " He brushes his knuckles gently across my cheek. "It reminds me of you."

I sigh as I bring my finger to trace the outline of his lips. "If I tell you you're romantic again, will you have to fuck me from behind to show how tough you are?"

He grins a wicked grin. "Maybe."

I see his wicked grin, and raise him a wink. "You are the most romantic man, and I love that you can quote poetry, and want it tattooed on your body."

"Now you've done it," he says in mock anger, making me giggle. "I'm going to show you what poetry-quoting men are made of."

"Sunshine and rose petals?"

"Piss and vinegar," he corrects. "And blood and sweat and pain…" He pauses, reaching out to twine my hair around his finger. "And locks of hair, from the only girl they ever loved."

My smile softens, and suddenly, my decision is made. "Let's do it. Let's leave tonight."

Gabe kisses the tip of my nose. "I'll book the flights as soon as I have the names on our new passports. But first, you and I need to do a photo shoot."

We get up and get dressed. Gabe takes my picture against the cream wall in the bathroom, before I take my turn, standing on top of an overturned trashcan so that I'll be tall enough to get a shot of him straight on. He sends the images to his contact, and gets an email back within a few minutes, saying that the documents will be ready later this afternoon. Gabe arranges to meet the man at Harry's diner at five o'clock with the money and gets the new names and birthdays for the plane tickets.

I sit on his lap as we book an eleven o'clock flight out of Charleston to Frankfurt, and then on to Pula, Croatia, where we'll rent a car to drive to the beach town of Porec. The flights are over a thousand dollars each, and when Gabe hits purchase, my stomach lurches.

"You just dropped eight thousand dollars on plane tickets" I say, still feeling queasy.

"It's only money," he says. "Speaking of, I need to get going. Kimmy has a friend who wants to buy the Beamer for ten grand. She's going to pick me up a few streets over in about ten minutes."

I frown. "Isn't that a lot less than it's worth?"

"It is." He shrugs. "But it's cash and it will be good to have some on hand while we're getting settled. And it's not like I can take the car with me." He stands, setting me on my feet. "Get the kids packed. I'll be back before dinner."

"Be careful, okay?" I hug him tight.

"You too," he says, kissing my forehead. "Try to lay low, but call me if there are any developments. I'll be back as soon as I can."

With one last squeeze, I reluctantly set him free. "I don't like the idea of being apart, even for a few hours."

"It's going to be okay," he says, backing toward the door. "We're almost home free, beautiful. Just hang on a little longer."

I smile as I watch him go, but when the door closes behind him, I can't help feeling like I'm never going to see him again.

CHAPTER
Sixteen

Caitlin

I stay busy for the next few hours—showering and changing into soft gray running shorts, and a black tee shirt, packing up the kids' backpacks, talking the boys through the plan, and arguing with Danny, who doesn't want to move to another country without at least getting to say goodbye to Sam in person—but I can't shake the sense of impending doom. When five-thirty comes and goes without a word from Gabe, I finally get so worried I pick up the phone.

My call is sent immediately to voicemail, but I try not to freak out. Gabe's contact might have been late to meet him at the diner;

they might still be in the middle of their exchange. There is probably some reasonable explanation for the delay.

I believe that, until the digital clock above the stove flicks to six, and three more calls go straight to voicemail. I'm about to tell Sherry that I'm going looking for Gabe, when my cell rings. I snatch it up from the counter where the kids are eating a subdued spaghetti dinner, my pulse racing with relief, only for my hopes to plummet when I see an unfamiliar number on the display.

It's not Gabe, but it's a local number, so I step into the bedroom and answer the call with a soft, "This is Caitlin."

"Hi, Caitlin," a familiar voice says. "This is Kimmy."

"Oh, hi Kimmy," I say, surprised. "What's up?"

"Listen, I know we're not friends or anything, but I didn't know who else to call, and Gabe left your number the other day with the keys, just in case there was an emergency with the car, and—"

"What's wrong?" I ask, the anxiety in Kimmy's voice making me impatient. "Is Gabe okay? Did something go wrong while you were selling the car?"

"No, that went fine," Kimmy says. "We got

everything taken care of, he got the money, and he went across the street to Harry's to meet a friend. I didn't expect to see him again, but then I realized he'd left his house key in the bowl by the door. I ran down to catch him before he left and I saw him leaving the diner with this super big guy. They were walking really close together and it just looked…weird, you know? And when I called Gabe's name, he didn't stop or turn around, and I know he had to have heard me. I was practically shouting."

"What did the guy look like?" I chew my thumbnail as I pace the carpet, fear that Gabe's father has intercepted him and forced him back to Darby Hill making my heart feel like it's punching my ribs. "Was he Gabe's height? An older man, with—"

"No, he was young," Kimmy says. "And taller and heavier than Gabe, with wider shoulders. I remember that, because you don't see many men bigger than Gabe."

Young, broad shoulders, bigger than Gabe….

A horrible suspicion sweeps through me, but I don't want to believe it's true. Still, I ask, "Did the man have light brown hair, a little curly at the bottom?"

"Yes," Kimmy says, sounding relieved,

though she has absolutely no reason to be. "Do you know him? Are he and Gabe friends?"

"What time did this happen?" I ignore her questions, knowing I don't have time to explain. There's a chance another massive guy with hair like Isaac's decided to take a close walk with Gabe out of the diner, but my gut says that's pretty unlikely.

"About an hour ago? Maybe a little less?"

"And you're just calling me now?" I ask, anger tightening my voice.

"It took me a while to get worried," Kimmy says, defensively. "And then I had to get up the guts to call you. It wasn't easy, okay. You *are* the woman he dumped me for."

I take a deep breath and rein in my temper. It's not Kimmy's fault something's happened to Gabe, and without her I might not have any clue where he is. "I'm sorry. I'm just worried. Can you tell me anything else? What direction they went? If they got into a car?"

Kimmy sighs. "They were walking down the street toward The Neptune and turned left on Mark Street, headed away from downtown. That's all I know."

"Thanks," I say. "I'll see if I can track him down."

"Do you need any help? I could take my

car and cruise one side of town while you cruise another."

"That's okay." I don't know what kind of situation I'll find, and I don't want Kimmy in the middle of something that might turn ugly. "But thanks. I appreciate the call."

"You're welcome," she says, then adds, "and let me know when you find him, will you? I'd like to know he's okay."

I promise to call her, hang up, and immediately call Isaac. But despite the fact that he's been leaving me angsty messages on and off for the past two days, Isaac doesn't pick up the phone, and when I'm transferred to voicemail, I get a message that his inbox is full. I hang up with a curse and stab out a quick text, telling Isaac to call me as soon as he gets my message. I tell him that I know he's in town, but I don't say anything about Gabe, not wanting to tip my hand on that just yet.

I send the text, and wait a few moments, but there are no happy "text in progress" bubbles from my ex-boyfriend. He seems to be lying low.

Or maybe he's too busy beating the shit out of Gabe to answer the phone.

The thought makes me shove my phone into the back pocket of my shorts and jog back into the other room. I tell the kids that I'm going out, and ask them to be good for Sherry, then pull Sherry aside long enough to explain where I'm going, and why.

"But what about the flight tonight?" she asks. "Should I still get the kids ready to go?"

I bite my lip, making the call on the spur of the moment. "Yes. If I'm not back by eight o'clock, call a cab to take everyone to the airport. Hopefully, Gabe and I will meet you there. If I get stuck, and won't be able to make it, and I'm able to call, I will."

"Why wouldn't you be able to call?" Sherry asks, skin paling beneath her freckles. "You don't think Isaac has gone off the deep end, do you?"

"I don't know." I don't want to scare her, but I want someone to know who might be responsible if I were to disappear along with Gabe. "But I'm going to be careful."

Sherry nods. "Do that. Be very careful, and call me as soon as you can."

"Will do." I lean in, giving her an impulsive hug. "Thank you. For everything."

"Go get your man," Sherry says, hugging me back. "And let's get you all on a plane before Aoife comes sniffing around and realizes you're making plans to flee the country."

LILI VALENTE

I told Sherry that the custody battle was the reason Gabe and I had decided to make the spur of the moment, international move. Because Sherry is my friend and knows I love Emmie like a daughter, she didn't doubt the story.

Still, I'm starting to feel all the lies I've told piling up around me, like concrete blocks stacked to the ceiling, ready to crash down and deliver life-threatening injuries. I need to get out of Giffney. I need to get to safety with Gabe and the kids, to a place where we can start fresh, and then maybe I can tell Sherry the truth. I want to be honest with the only friend I have left, but right now isn't the time.

"Call soon," I promise, pulling away and starting toward the door, grabbing the keys off the counter as I go.

Minutes later, I'm in the parking lot, heading for the rental van, so focused on puzzling out where Isaac might have taken Gabe that I don't notice the silver Camry parked a few spots away until my sister steps out and slams the door. I increase my speed, hoping to get into the van and out of the parking lot before Aoife can trap me, but she moves fast for a pregnant woman.

She's by my side by the time I reach the door, covering my hand with hers.

CHAPTER
Seventeen

Caitlin

*"And each man stands with his face in the light of his own drawn sword.
Ready to do what a hero can."*
-Elizabeth Barrett Browning

"We have to talk." Aoife's voice is low, urgent, and her grip on my hand firm enough to make it obvious she hasn't come here to mess around.

"I don't have time right now." I try to pull my hand free, but Aoife doesn't let go. Her fingers dig into mine as she steps closer, until I can smell her gardenia perfume, the same brand she's worn since we were little girls, and

Gram gave her a bottle for her birthday.

The smell sends melancholy oozing through my chest. What would Gram think of us now? The little girls she always said were like two angels fallen from heaven, we were both so beautiful and sweet.

"You need to make time," Aoife says. "Gabe's dad came to the funeral today."

"I know." I lift my chin, meeting her hard gaze straight on, playing tough, though my pulse is pounding with fear.

"He asked me to stop by his office after we finished at the gravesite," she says, her grip still firm on my hand. "He said he wanted to give me something that would make sure I got full custody of Emmie."

I tighten my jaw, willing my expression not to falter. "And? Did he?"

"He did," she says, her own expression unreadable. "He showed me footage of you breaking into someone's house. At first I couldn't be sure it was you, but the person who was filming followed the van and caught you taking off your mask."

I close my eyes, not wanting Aoife to see me crumble. This is what Gabe and I were afraid of, this is why we were getting ready to run. But fearing something, and having the hard evidence shoved in your face, are two very different things, and it suddenly feels like all those concrete blocks are tumbling down on top of me, after all.

"He had a private detective following you and Gabe," Aoife continues. "He caught you breaking into two different houses, but Aaron cut all the footage of Gabe out on the DVD he gave to me. He told me to use it to blackmail you into giving up Emmie. He doesn't want this going to court because he knows you might testify that Gabe was your partner."

I open my eyes, confused by the compassionate note in my sister's voice. "So…are you going to blackmail me? Is that why you're here?"

Aoife's fingers tighten, until her grip on my hand is almost painful. "Aaron Alexander told me today that *you* are the reason his son started committing crimes, but I know that's not true."

"You do?" I squint into the sun turning my sister's hair into a golden halo, trying to get a better look at her face. I would swear she looks upset, but I have no idea why. This is exactly what she wanted, handed to her on a silver platter.

"Because I know it's *my* fault," she says, her face crumpling. "And I'm so sorry."

I blink in shock, but I don't have time to speak before Aoife continues in a teary voice—

"I know how hard it was just looking after the boys without Mom around, and I left you with the boys *and* a newborn and nobody in the world to help you." She releases my hand to swipe the tears from her cheeks. "At first I was so fucked up I didn't even think about what I'd done, but then I talked myself into believing it was okay. You've always been so much stronger than me. I told myself you could handle it and—"

"But I'm not...I wasn't," I say, the words bursting from my chest though I know I don't have time to hash through our family drama right now. "You were always the one I turned to, Aoife. Always. Ever since I was a baby. I would have died without you. I loved you and counted on you and I...." I press my lips together, but I can't seem to stop myself from finishing my sentence. "I fucking worshipped you, Aoife, and you *left* me."

I fight through the wave of emotion, refusing to cry, or let her see just how deep this goes. This is a wound that cuts through flesh and bone, slicing straight into the soft center of my heart, where all my feelings for the big sister I once loved so much have been locked away.

"I know," she says, fresh tears spilling from her blue eyes. "I'm so sorry. I know it's my fault that you had to start stealing. I know if I'd stayed, or at least sent money home when I could, you might not have had to do what you did. You were right today, I can't erase the past, no matter how much I want to."

"Me either," I say in a soft voice. "I can't go back and undo what I did last summer, but I promise you it isn't as bad as it looks. I did steal things, but I stole from criminals Gabe's dad helped keep out of jail. That doesn't excuse it, but I want you to know I wasn't hurting innocent people. That's not who I am."

She nods. "I'm not here to judge what you did. I'm here to say I'm sorry, and to warn you that Gabe's dad is going to turn the footage over to the police tomorrow morning."

My breath rushes out. "Why? I thought you said he didn't want to risk me testifying against Gabe."

"He gave me today to convince you to give me Emmie, break things off with Gabe, and leave town," she says. "If Gabe isn't home, and you on a plane to somewhere else by tomorrow morning, Mr. Alexander is going to the police. I think he thinks you and Gabe might run if he gives you too much time."

He thinks right. And we might still escape if I can find Gabe, and get to the airport before it's too late.

"He's scared of his son ending up in jail," Aoife continues, "but he seems more scared of losing him."

"He's scared of losing control," I say bitterly. "That's all he's ever wanted."

Aoife casts a glance over her shoulder before turning back to me. "You may be right, but whether he's motivated by love, or something else, he seems determined. You and the kids should get out of here as soon as you can."

My chest loosens, but I'm afraid to trust that I understand what she's saying. "But what about the court date on Friday?"

"I'm dropping my suit," she says, crossing her arms over her chest. "I don't want to hurt Emmie. It's going to kill me, but at least I'll know I did what's best for my daughter. She loves you. You're her real mother. I'm just an egg donor, like you said."

I wouldn't have believed it possible an hour ago, but at that moment, all the love I ever felt for my big sister, my protector, my friend, comes rushing back, so big and strong, I can't keep myself from leaning in and wrapping my arms around her. "You don't have to lose her," I say. "We can work something out. You can come see her; you can be close. Maybe...*we* can be close again, too."

"I would like that." Aoife's arms go around me. She hugs me and her baby bump presses against my stomach, reminding me I have another niece on the way.

"The baby is going to be her half sister," I say. "They should be close, too."

"No, the baby will be her cousin," Aoife says, smiling when I pull back to look in her eyes. "And I'll be Aunt Aoife."

I nod, but the smile teasing at my lips vanishes before it can fully form. "I have to go. I'm sorry, but I really do."

Aoife gives my shoulders a squeeze before she steps back. "Okay. Call me when you can, and let me know when you get settled."

"We aren't going back to Hawaii," I say, reaching for the door, knowing I need to go, but feeling I should at least give Aoife a heads up. "We can't. Not with Gabe's dad determined to do what he's going to do."

Aoife smiles that savvy, been-around-the-block smile I remember so well. "I figured. Just don't go to Mexico. The actually do extradite people every now and then, if someone slips the police enough money."

"Got it." I capture her hand for one last squeeze. "And thank you. I love you."

"I love you, too," she says, voice trembling. "Now get going, before I start crying again."

I get into the van and start it up. Aoife moves to stand in the grass on the parking median, watching me go with a peaceful expression on her face. I never expected her to do the right thing, but she did. It gives me hope that maybe—once I find Isaac and Gabe—it won't be as bad a scene as I'm fearing.

Maybe Isaac just wanted to talk to Gabe. Or to apologize. I listened to all the messages he left. He seemed truly sorry, devastated that he'd hurt me, and willing to do whatever it takes to make things better. Maybe he wanted to make things better with Gabe, too.

"And maybe my dad's going to come back as a leprechaun and tell me where he's hidden his pot of gold," I mutter to myself as I drive up and down the streets of downtown, hunting for some sign of Isaac and Gabe, and coming up empty.

Isaac doesn't want to make nice with Gabe. Isaac is jealous of Gabe. He *hates* Gabe. He blames him for turning sweet, pliable Caitlin into a stubborn woman with hard edges, and no mercy for her enemies.

But Isaac hasn't begun to see my merciless side. If he's hurt Gabe, he's going to get a very close, very personal introduction.

I drive past Isaac's dad's pizza place, but there's no sign of him or Gabe through the front windows, or in the alley behind the restaurant. I drive by Isaac's parents' house and his old apartment, but the windows are dark at the house and the apartment is occupied by a young couple I can see watching television on the couch through the window. I drive by every other old stomping ground I can think of, until it's after eight, and I'm genuinely starting to freak out that I won't find Gabe in time.

Finally, I steer the van back toward my old side of town, on the off chance that Isaac has decided to take Gabe to his piece of shit brother's house on Cooper Street, but I'm not optimistic about my chances of finding him there. Isaac hates Gabe, but I'm pretty sure he hates his brother, Ian, more. Ian did time in prison, and has mooched off their parents ever since he got out, not even making an effort to find a job. He's stolen money from Isaac, wrecked Isaac's first car that he worked an entire summer to buy, and refused to go to his own grandmother's funeral because he was too hungover.

I feel pretty confident saying that Isaac would rather ask for help from the devil himself than his little brother, but when I pull up in front of the dingy duplex on Cooper Street, the lights are on inside, and two shadows are moving back and forth behind the curtained windows.

One of them is tall and broad, and the other is even taller and broader because the Ronconis make big, meaty boys.

I slow the van. I don't see a Gabe-shaped shadow, but something instinctive tells me he's inside. All the hairs on my arms stand on end, my heart starts beating faster, and I just *know* he's close.

And that he's in trouble.

I continue down the street for another two blocks before I pull over and cut the engine. Ian doesn't live in the best neighborhood, but I decide to leave the keys in the ignition, anyway. Hopefully, I won't be away from the car very long, and I may need to make a swift getaway. If Ian and Isaac both try to stop me, my only advantage will be speed. They're both big enough to lift me over their heads with one arm tied behind their backs.

I hurry down the street, clinging to the shadows, wishing I were wearing my blacks.

My tee shirt is black, but I'm sure my pale hair is glowing in the soft moonlight and my bare legs stand out in the darkness, despite my tan. But hopefully Ian and Isaac won't be looking out any of the windows when I creep by.

When I reach the yard, I bend over, moving quickly and quietly past the window, and the front porch, where a collection of empty beer bottles litters the stoop. I figure it's best to be careful though, from the looks of things, Isaac and Ian are still standing with their backs to the window, in the middle of an animated discussion. Now that I'm closer, I hear raised voices, though I can't make out what they're saying. But Ian doesn't sound happy, and neither does Isaac.

Still, that's nothing new. Ian and Isaac have been arguing since the day Ian learned to talk. It doesn't mean that Isaac has brought a hostage to Ian's house, and asked his brother to help him pound his girlfriend's ex into a bloody lump of flesh. This could be a normal Ronconi brother fight, and I could have misjudged the entire situation.

I let the thought temper my nerves, but I don't believe it, and when I reach the side of the duplex and stand on tiptoe to gaze through the window above the kitchen sink, I'm not surprised to see Gabe sitting in one of

Ian's kitchen chairs, with his hands tied behind him. His back is to me, so I can't see his face, but he's sitting up straight, and his shoulders are square. It looks like he's still okay. For now.

My heart does a giddy flip in my chest. I want to call out to him so badly it hurts, but I don't say a word. I can't risk attracting Ian's or Isaac's attention until I have a plan for getting Gabe out.

I let my eyes trail back and forth from one end of the dingy kitchen to the other, and into what I can see of the living room beyond. It looks like the front door must open into the living room, but there is a hall leading out of the kitchen to the left. I suspect it leads to the bedroom and bathroom, and that there must be a back door somewhere. I'm about to go hunting for it, when Ian strides into the kitchen, a furious look on his face, and a gun in his hand.

Heart pounding, I spin to my right, gluing my back against the side of the house and peering into the kitchen over my shoulder. But I can't see much from this angle, and all I can think about is that gun in Ian's hand. That gun, Gabe tied up and helpless, and Ian and Isaac free to do whatever they want to the man I love.

I would never in a million years have dreamed that Isaac would try to kill Gabe— threaten him, beat him up, throw our relationship in his face, yes, but not *kill* him. I don't know if the gun is Ian's and things have gotten out of hand, or if Isaac planned to bring Gabe here and eliminate his competition forever, but I know that I can't wait for the ideal moment to present itself. I have to act fast and think even faster, if I'm going to be sure Gabe leaves this house in one piece.

Remembering the collection of beer bottles on the stoop, I move swiftly away from the window, adrenaline dumping into my veins as I put my barely formed plan into motion.

A LOVE SO DEEP

CHAPTER
Eighteen

Gabe

"The web of our life is of a mingled yarn, good
and ill together:
our virtues would be proud, if our faults
whipp'd them not;
and our crimes would despair, if they were not
cherish'd by our virtues."
-Shakespeare

Once, when I was a little boy, so young I probably shouldn't be able to remember anything about this particular incident, I wet my pants while my mother and I were at a rare play date at our closest neighbors' house. I don't remember what the other little boy and I were playing, only that it was fascinating and I didn't want to stop playing it, and so I kept putting off going to the bathroom until it was too late.

My mother was horribly embarrassed. She apologized a hundred times, all while dragging me, in my soggy pants, out the door. We arrived home in a few minutes, but instead of sending for my nanny to give me a bath the way she normally would, my mother took me around the house to the garden and sat me down in one of the wrought iron chairs near her rose bushes. She told me I was going to sit in that chair for a time out until my pants were dry, extra time in my wet britches being my punishment for having an accident in public.

Even though I wasn't even four years old, I remember that it was the "in public" part that seemed to bother my mother the most. She felt that I'd made a fool of her in front of her friend. I'd put a crack in the Alexander family image, and she was angry and ashamed and willing to make a three-year-old sit in his urine-soaked clothes for over an hour to teach me a lesson about what was expected of me when I was in front of other people.

I know that's why she and my father did what they did last summer.

Why they hired a private detective to follow

me when I started acting out of character, going against my many years of Alexander training. I was too old to sit in a chair, but they weren't willing to risk leaving me to my own devices. They were afraid their terminally ill, unstable son might do something to embarrass them, and they wanted to be prepared to run damage control.

They never imagined the PI would bring back footage of me, and my new girlfriend, breaking into the houses of Dad's former clients and stealing things. They blamed Caitlin, of course. Mom said she was trash, Dad said she was a criminal like her grandfather, who was relatively famous around Giffney for petty theft. I insisted that I was the one who had seduced Caitlin into breaking the rules, but they wouldn't believe me. They were going to take the footage of Caitlin to the police, unless I agreed to the surgery.

I made them swear they would destroy it. I swore I would come back from the grave, and haunt them if they broke the promise. Then I got on the fucking plane to Michigan. I couldn't see any other choice that wouldn't result in Caitlin and me both ending up in jail. While that wouldn't have meant much to a man with a brain tumor, Caitlin had her whole life in front of her. I only had a few weeks, at best.

The memories all came back to me in a heady rush, while I was walking away from Harry's diner with a gun pressed against my side. I remembered everything about that last day in Giffney, right down to the way I'd cried as the plane took off, even though my father was sitting next to me.

I wasn't in any shape to fight for Caitlin then, but I am now, and I have given myself permission to do whatever I have to do to get out of this kitchen alive. I'm going to bide my time, get my hands on the gun the younger brother keeps shifting from hand to hand, and make sure neither one of these Neanderthals can follow me when I leave this house.

I'll try to let them live if I can, but if I can't...

Isaac said he isn't planning to kill me, as long as I cooperate, but I saw his finger whiten on the trigger when I reached for the door handle a little too quickly when we pulled up in his brother's driveway. He's looking for an excuse. I'm not sure even *he's* aware of it, but I see the blood lust in his eyes.

He hates me for winning the heart of the girl he says he's loved since he was a child, but what he feels for Caitlin isn't love. He would destroy every beautiful, fierce, passionate thing about her. Caitlin isn't a woman you fence in; she's a woman you set free, and run like hell to keep up with her.

But Isaac doesn't understand. He's insisting on "protecting" Caitlin from the big bad rich boy who led her down the garden path. The same way my parents have insisted on moving heaven and earth to protect me from the "trash," who they believe tempted me into a life of crime. What none of them realize is that there is no one to blame. There is just Caitlin and me, two people who made some brave choices, and some bad choices, and fell in love along the way. Neither of us is perfect or blameless, but sometimes two imperfect people can make one perfect love.

Since Caitlin walked back into my life, I don't hate myself anymore. I'm not the man my parents want me to be, or the type of guy who will ever be embraced by people who see the world in black and white. But for people who see the shades of gray, and who understand that there is comfort to be found in the shadows, I have something to give.

I helped Caitlin get a fair shot for the first time in her life, and she paid it forward in her life without me. We've helped people, and will continue to help people, and along the way we're going to raise some kids together. We're going to love them and listen to them and let them make mistakes—in public, and in private—and we will try to help them grow up the best we can.

That future is all I want, all I will ever want, and no one is going to take it—or Caitlin—away from me.

Moments after the thought flickers through my head, the younger brother, Ian—a seemingly perpetually irritated man dressed in threadbare jeans, a Mountain Dew tee shirt, with oily brown hair, and small, angry eyes that make him look like an uglier, near-sighted version of his older brother—comes storming into the kitchen, waving his gun.

"You haven't thought this shit through," he says in a low rumble, his voice deeper than Isaac's due to the pack a day habit that has helped make his house smell like a garlic-and-ash scented armpit.

"I have," Isaac says from the living room. "I'm telling you, this is going to be fine. They'd do anything for him. They bought Caitlin a house in Maui just to get her out of town, for God's sake."

"You should get them to buy *you* a house," Ian says, scowling around the kitchen, looking anywhere but directly at me.

LILI VALENTE

No matter how big and bad he is, when I walked inside, he took one look into my eyes, and hasn't made eye contact since. He's a fool, but he's smarter than his brother. Isaac doesn't have the sense to know when he's caught a shark with his minnow net.

"I don't want a house." Isaac sounds more exhausted than he did the last time he explained this. "I told you. I want them to give me all of the copies of that tape they say they have of Caitlin committing a crime. If they even have one. I wouldn't put it past them to lie. They're crazy."

"You're the one who took their plane ticket to Maui," Ian says. "Mom's still pissed at you, by the way. Family comes first, and you left Dad a chef short when you ran off."

"Caitlin is my family, too." Isaac comes to stand in the doorway, causing his fidgety brother to shift the gun from his left hand to his right, and move close enough to where I'm tied that I think I could get my teeth into his wrist before he has a chance to raise the weapon.

Once he drops it, I'll fall on top, and do my best to grab the gun with my bound hands and fire it. It doesn't matter what I hit, as long as I don't hit myself. The gunshot will be enough to ensure the police are called, and,

207

I'm hoping, enough to convince Ian and Isaac that their plan is going south, and it's best to cut and run while they still can.

Or they could flip out, fight you for the gun, and shoot you.

They could, but if I don't get to Caitlin and get on that flight out tonight, the chances of us escaping aren't looking good. Now that I've remembered what my parents used to blackmail me, I know Caitlin is in real danger. I doubt Aaron and Deborah will go straight to the police—they'll try to blackmail Caitlin first—but if all else fails, I wouldn't put it past my parents to involve the authorities.

They want me back the way I was before the tumor diagnosis, or they don't want me at all. I sincerely believe they'd rather see me rotting in jail than spending my newly-released trust fund on Caitlin Cooney and her family. They raised me to be the prince of this town, not to run off into the Croatian sunset with the daughter of the town drunk.

They aren't going to pull any punches, and neither can I. I need to get back to Caitlin. Tonight. And if risking a gunshot wound is the only way to do it, so be it.

I'm tensing my leg muscles, preparing to launch myself from my chair and sink my teeth deep into Ian's wrist, when a huge crash—like the contents of a recycling bin being dumped onto concrete—sounds from outside on the porch. Ian curses and strides across the room to join Isaac in the doorway, taking him, and his wrist, out of reach.

"Fuck," Ian says, shoving Isaac toward the front door. "Check outside. The only reason anyone would be poking around here is because of you."

Isaac looks like he's going to protest, but in the end he just rolls his eyes. "Fine. But it was probably a cat or dog or something. I told you, no one followed me here."

He's right. No one did, because I was driving while he held a gun on me, and I was paying close attention. We weren't followed, and I honestly didn't think there was a chance in hell anyone would find me here, at least not anytime soon.

But I should have known better than to underestimate my girl.

When Caitlin rushes through the hallway leading to the back of the house, and bashes Ian over the head with the base of a lamp while his back is turned, I can't say I'm *that* surprised. I'm relieved, proud, and grateful that this is the woman I'm going to spend the rest of my life with, but not surprised.

Ian crumples to the ground with a groan. A

second later, his gun is in Caitlin's hand. A moment after that, Isaac rushes back into the room, and Caitlin lifts the gun, aiming it at her ex-best-friend's chest.

CHAPTER
Nineteen

Caitlin

*"If thou must love me, let it be for nought
Except for love's sake only. Do not say,
'I love her for her smile—her look—her way
Of speaking gently.'"*
-Elizabeth Barrett Browning

I hold the gun steady, shaking my head when Isaac takes a step toward me. "Don't move, or I'll shoot you. I swear to God I will." I reach down, feeling around Ian's neck until I find a pulse, and stand up as soon as I make sure he's alive. I never expected to knock him out, but I guess I underestimated my own strength.

Just like Isaac.

"Caitlin, please," Isaac says. "You don't understand." He lifts his big hands into the air—the same hands he used to slip beneath my tee shirt, when he knew that Gabe was alive, and the only man I wanted to be with— and takes another step.

I slide the action and drop the barrel of the gun, shifting my aim from his chest to his crotch. "Or maybe I'll shoot you there. Make the punishment fit the crime."

"You don't mean that," he says, but sweat breaks out on his upper lip, and he doesn't take another step.

"Try me," I say, not taking my eyes off of him. "Are you all right, Gabe?"

"Now that you're here, beautiful, I'm perfect," he says, sounding so pleased and proud of me it would make me smile, if I weren't staring into the face of the person who has betrayed me more completely than any other.

My mom and dad were supposed to be the people I could trust the most, but from day one, I knew that was a fairy tale that was never going to come true. Even Aoife came home fucked up often enough at the end that it wasn't a complete shock when she ran off. But Isaac was always someone I could count on, the big, cuddly bear of a best friend who had my back, and never let me down. And he lied to me worse than any of them. Because he made me believe he was truly one of the good guys.

"I'm going to untie Gabe," I tell Isaac, venom in every word. "I think I'd enjoy causing you pain, right now, so stay right there, and don't give me an excuse to shoot you."

I move slowly, keeping the gun trained on Isaac as I cross the room, using my peripheral vision to guide me closer to Gabe's chair.

"Please, let me explain," Isaac begs, sweat beading on his brow to join the drops forming on his upper lip. "I know this looks bad, but I'm doing this for you. Gabe's parents said they have surveillance videos of you committing a crime. They're going to use it to put you in jail if—"

"I know about the footage." I reach Gabe's side and rest a hand on his shoulder, just that brief touch enough to give me strength. He's okay. He's really okay. I'm not too late. "Gabe's parents hired a private investigator to follow me and Gabe last summer."

Isaac's eyes widen. "Then it's true?" He shakes his head, grief twisting his features as I work on the knots binding Gabe's arms with my free hand. "God, Caitlin, what has he done to you? Can't you see how bad this relationship has been for you and the kids? Please, let me help. Leave him tied up. We can call his parents, ransom him for the video, and then get the hell out of here. We can start over and—"

"I don't think that's a good idea," Gabe says, in a silky voice. "I mean, talk about bad influences, I doubt you've kidnapped anyone at gun point before now. Seems to me this obsession with Caitlin has been bad for *you*, Isaac. Best for you to get some professional help, and let this dream go. Because, as I'm sure Caitlin will tell you, you're never getting your sweaty paws on her again."

Isaac scowls, and his hands ball into fists. "Shut your mouth, you fucking piece of—"

"Quiet, Isaac," I say, in a sharp tone. "You too, Gabe."

"What?" Gabe asks, innocence personified. "I'm just trying to be helpful."

"You're poking the bear, and you know it," I say, fighting the urge to smile when Gabe laughs.

"You're sick," Isaac says, glaring at Gabe with enough heat to melt his skin from his bones. "You're the one who needs professional help. You've ruined her life!"

"No one has ruined my life," I say,

abandoning the knots and standing with a frustrated sigh. "I'm not going to be able to get the ropes untied with the gun in my hand, and I'm not taking the gun off of you, Isaac. So I want you to cross the kitchen, slowly, kneel down, and untie Gabe. If you try to hurt him, or make any sudden moves, I will shoot you, please don't make me prove that, okay?"

"He doesn't believe you're capable," Gabe says, turning his head to look at me for the first time. I feel his attention on my face, and know he's truly worried. "Be careful."

"I will be," I tell him. "I'll shoot if I have to. I'm leaving here with you, Gabe, and nothing and no one is going to stop me." I motion with the gun. "Let's go, Isaac, nice and slow."

Isaac starts across the room, and I back away, maintaining a good six feet between us, so that if he lunges for the gun, I'll have time to react. I keep the gun trained on his torso and my eyes on his face, sensing that—should he decide to try something—I'll see it in his eyes, before I'll see it in his body language.

"Please, Caitlin," he begs as he moves. "Please don't do this. I love you so much. It feels like I've loved you my entire life."

"It isn't love when it's built on a lie, Isaac," I say, my stomach clenching at the desperation in his voice. I would feel sorry for him, but the second he threatened Gabe, my pity went out the window. Now, I just want to get away from him. Forever.

"Not everything was a lie," he says. "We were happy together for a while. You know we were, you know we—"

"I don't know anything, except that the sight of you is making me sick." I make my tone as heartless as I can, not wanting to give Isaac even a shred of hope that this bargaining is working. "Now stop talking, and get to work. I don't want to hear another word from you until Gabe's arms are free."

Isaac grimaces, but he doesn't speak again. He shuffles around behind Gabe's chair, hands trembling and more sweat rolling from his body. By the time he kneels down, his face is covered in beads of perspiration. Sweat drips from his temples and chin, but his skin is pale and sallow, not flushed the way it is after a run.

He looks awful, and if I didn't know better, I'd think he'd been using drugs. He reminds me of Aoife, when she'd come home itching and sweating, dying for a fix after her boyfriend of the moment had run out of money or moved on to the next pretty girl with a bad habit. But Isaac is so straight he only rarely drinks on Saturday night. The fix he craves is something you can't buy on a street corner, and he knows he's never getting his hands on it again. And that's the kind of thing that makes a junkie desperate.

I know that. I've been around enough people with monkeys on their backs to know they'll do crazy things to feed their addictions. I should have known Isaac wasn't going to play nice, but when he turns and rushes me, using every bit of muscle in his long, powerful legs, I'm not prepared.

I hesitate a beat too long.

"Caitlin!" Gabe calls out my name in warning, but it's too late, I'm already in the air, my back slamming into the wall behind me.

I groan as the back of my head bounces off the plaster, but I hold tight to the gun and pull my elbow down toward my ribs, wedging the weapon in between me and Isaac as he pins me to the wall with his body.

"I'm sorry, I'm sorry," he says, even as his hands tighten around my waist until it feels like his fingers are going to puncture my skin. "I don't want to hurt you. I never wanted to hurt you."

"Then put me down, and don't make me have to shoot you. My finger is still on the trigger," I say through gritted teeth, hating the feel of his sweaty body flush against mine, and the sour smell of his breath hot on my face. The last of the affection I feel for Isaac is rapidly transforming into contempt, but I still don't want to shoot him unless I have no other choice.

"Put her down, Isaac," Gabe says from the kitchen. "She's half your size. If you want to fight, come untie me, and we can fight. Just you and me, out in the yard with our fists, until one of us drops."

"Shut up," Isaac shouts, making me flinch. "I'm sorry," he adds in a whisper. "I just hate him, Caitlin. I hate his voice, I hate his face, I hate his money, and his fucking cocky attitude. And I hate that you love him…more than you love me." He sucks in a breath that emerges as a sob. "Why, Caitlin? Why don't you love me?"

I stare up into his glassy eyes, with all the pain simmering behind them, but I know Isaac isn't looking back at me. He isn't seeing *me*, he's seeing whatever it is that has left him so broken he doesn't have the love for himself he needs to let me go. Maybe it's because his parents always favored Ian, even though his little brother was an unrepentant asshole. Maybe it's all those years of being called "Titty Boy" in elementary school, back before Isaac became an athlete, and was just big and overweight, not big and strong. Maybe it's because his last girlfriend, Heather, told him he was lousy in bed when they broke up, and swore she had never loved him.

Maybe it's a little of all those things, but looking up at him now, I know it wouldn't matter if I promised to go back to Maui with him, and love him forever. It wouldn't matter if there had never been a Gabe, and Isaac had been my first and only. Isaac would never be confident in my love. He would still do his best to wear me down, and keep me weak, because that's the only way he knows how to be strong. All these years I thought he was my rock, but really he was picking away at my foundation, so that he would always need to be there to prop me up.

"That's not the answer you need, Isaac," I finally say, though I doubt anything I say will make a difference with him in his current state. "You need to ask why you don't love yourself."

Isaac sobs and drops his head, bringing his sweaty cheek to press against mine. "I need you, Caitlin. Please don't leave. Please stay with me. I'll be whatever you want me to be. I'll make a lot of money. I'll learn to walk and talk like a cocky asshole, whatever you need. Just please stay. Please let me take you away from here, and keep you safe."

Lock me away is more like it. Isaac doesn't want a partner, he wants a princess in a tower, always in need of rescuing. We are trapped in a tug of war between what Isaac needs, and who I am, and only one of us is going to win. I know that, and I suddenly know he's not going to give me a choice whether or not to pull the trigger.

"I'm going to shoot you, Isaac," I say, tears filling my eyes. "If you don't put me down and walk away, right now, I'm going to shoot you."

He shakes his head. "You won't. I know you won't."

I swallow past the lump in my throat and curl my finger. "You're wrong. If you could really see me, you would know that."

The gunshot is so loud it feels like a thunderbolt has ripped through my head. Isaac drops me and stumbles back, clutching the top of his shoulder, his mouth open wide, but I can't hear his scream. All I can hear is high-pitched whining in my ears, and the pounding of my blood rushing through my veins. I slide the action again and aim the gun at Isaac, but he's already on the floor, clutching his bleeding shoulder as he curls into a sobbing ball on the linoleum. The wound doesn't look fatal, but the fact that I've shot him seems to have killed the last of Isaac's will to fight for me. I wait another beat, long enough to make sure he's staying down, and then I hurry across the room to free Gabe.

Gabe's mouth moves, but I can't hear him, either, so I just shake my head and kneel down. I set the gun between my knees and work the knots free in less than a minute now that I have the use of both of my hands.

Gabe springs up from the chair, pulling me up off the ground and hugging me tight. He smoothes my hair from my forehead, and I think I hear him mumble something, but I still can't make out the words.

"I can't hear you," I say, looking up into his steady blue eyes. "My ears are ringing. But we have to get out of here. Should we bring the gun?"

Gabe shakes his head, then presses the rope I pulled from his wrists into my hand before motioning to Ian on the ground. I nod, and kneel down next to Isaac's brother, pulling his heavy arms behind his back and binding them, doing my best not to look at Isaac writhing on the floor a few feet away.

I'm dimly aware of Gabe moving around the kitchen, doing something with the gun, but I don't look up until he kneels next to Isaac and rolls him over onto his back.

Isaac's scream as he's moved is loud enough to penetrate the ringing filling my head, but he doesn't fight Gabe when Gabe presses a folded kitchen towel to his shoulder, then wraps a garbage bag around it, and ties it tight, ensuring there will be pressure on the wound. Once he's finished, Gabe moves to Isaac's feet and tugs the laces from his boots before using them to tie Isaac's legs together.

When he's finished, he presses another towel into my hands and makes wiping gestures. I nod and begin striding swiftly around the kitchen, wiping down everything I think I touched. Gabe does the same with another towel, and in a few minutes, he's back at my side, urging me down the darkened hall to the back door.

"We...go," he says. "No sirens...but...soon."

I pick up pieces of his sentences as the ringing in my ears begins to fade, and nod. "Let's go. The keys are in the van. It's parked two blocks away."

I follow him down the hall, ignoring the pitiful voice calling my name from behind me.

Isaac is in my past now. He's going to live, and I'm glad about that, but in my heart he's dead and buried. I don't have any more love to waste on him.

I'm saving my energy for Gabe, the kids, and the new life waiting for us if Gabe and I can make it to the airport in time.

A LOVE SO DEEP

CHAPTER
Twenty

Gabe

*"But shall I live in hope? All men, I hope,
live so."*
-Shakespeare

Caitlin and I make it to the airport with only fifteen minutes remaining before the flight to Frankfurt will begin to board. Luckily, the rental car office is closed, and all we have to do is park the van, dump the keys in a lockbox, and catch the shuttle to the terminal. Even luckier, I have all our passports and birth certificates, and ten grand in cash from the sale of the car, shoved into my back pockets. I tucked it all into my jeans on the way out of Harry's, and the documents aren't much worse for wear after my adventure with Isaac.

Caitlin and I step off the shuttle, and jog hand in hand toward the international terminal, with eight minutes left before our flight is due to board. Just from the way her palm is sweating in mine, I can tell she's starting to stress. Big time.

"I'll get the boarding passes," I say as we hurry through the automatic doors. "You say goodbye to Sherry, and get the kids ready to go through security."

She nods and gives my hand one final squeeze before we part ways—me toward the self-serve kiosks, and her toward an anxious-looking Sherry, who is holding a sleeping Emmie in her arms. In the next row of seats, Ray and Sean lean tiredly against each other, a pile of backpacks at their feet. Caitlin and I agreed the kids should only bring their essentials, no suitcases. The lighter we travel, the more quickly we can move, and we can always buy new clothes and toys when we get to Porec.

I print out the boarding passes and tuck each pass into the corresponding passport, hoping I'm saving us time, and that the kids are going to remember their new names just in case someone asks. Emmie, at least, looks too far gone to do more than drool on my shoulder as we pass through security, but hopefully Caitlin's talk with the boys this afternoon made an impression. I know Ray and Sean are tough, but they've been through a lot the past year, and God only knows when the next stressful situation is going to be the one that breaks them.

The only person I'm not worried about is Caitlin, who was a champion through the entire ordeal with Isaac, and started the van with a steady hand a minute after we left the house. Gone is the trembling, shattered woman who had trouble holding it together after Ned Pitt almost killed her. I don't know if it's the fact that Isaac is obviously going to live, or that Caitlin is simply that much tougher than she was before, but I can tell she's already put our interlude with Isaac behind her and moved on, her focus on the future.

I couldn't be prouder of her, and I can't wait to get on that plane tonight. I'll breathe easier as soon as we touch down in Frankfurt, and have a few thousand miles, and an ocean, between her and my parents.

"We ready?" I ask as I reach Caitlin and Sherry, who are talking in whispers so as not to wake Emmie. "Is everything okay?"

Caitlin turns, driving a hand through her hair. "No. Danny ran off."

"What?" I ask, glancing around the terminal, wondering where he could have gone.

"It was at the hotel," Sherry clarifies in a tone that makes it clear she feels terrible for losing one of the kids. "He went to get snacks from the machine down the hall, and didn't come back for a long time. Then Ray found a note in the bathroom. Danny said he's not coming with you guys tonight. He wants to fly back to Maui with me next Tuesday to say good-bye to Sam, and then meet you after. He promised he'd come back to the hotel tomorrow morning after y'all were gone."

"I should have known something like this would happen," Caitlin says, teeth digging into her bottom lip hard enough to turn the skin white. "He let me off the hook way too easy this afternoon when I told him we weren't going back to Hawaii." She curses softly. "God, that kid. What are we going to do?"

"We're going to get on the plane," I say, glancing at Sherry. "Assuming you're okay with taking Danny back to Maui with you next week?"

Sherry nods. "Totally. I don't mind at all,

and he can stay with me and Bjorn until you guys book another flight for him. Danny and I get along great, I just feel so bad."

"Don't feel bad," Caitlin says, squeezing Sherry's arm before turning back to me. "But I don't know, Gabe. What if something happens and we can't get him to Croatia to meet us? What will we do then?"

"We'll figure something out," I say, adding gently. "And he's a smart kid, he's going to take care of himself tonight, and come back to Sherry tomorrow the way he promised. But if we don't get going, we might not make the flight, and we're not guaranteed another chance out of the country."

Caitlin filled me in on her sister's warning on the way to the airport. She knows the danger is real, and after only a moment, she nods.

"Okay, let's go." She grabs Emmie's backpack and her own from the ground. "Ray, Sean, grab your bags, guys, we've got to hustle to make it on the plane."

"I want pretzels," Sean says sleepily. "Will they have free pretzels on this one?"

"I'll buy you pretzels from the stewardess if they don't," I say, leaning down so that Sherry can more easily shift Emmie into my arms. Emmie snuffles and turns her cheek the other direction on my shoulder, but doesn't wake up, and thirty seconds later we've waved good-bye to Sherry and started toward security.

At ten-fifteen on a Monday night, the security line in the international terminal is nearly deserted. Mr. and Mrs. Lawrence Clement and their sleepy daughter, Sophie—as well as Mrs. Clement's two younger brothers, Derrick and Henry Dawes—are swept through the family line in just a few minutes, spared the ordeal of having to remove shoes by a quick sweep of Mr. Clement's palms, proving he hasn't been tampering with any chemicals or explosives in his recent past. (Though it's a good thing they didn't sweep Mrs. Clement, instead, as she might have had gun powder residue clinging to her skin.)

The Clement clan reach their gate with a few minutes left to spare, and take their place at the end of the long line waiting to board the plane to Frankfurt. Seeing an opportunity to obtain the pretzels he promised his young brother-in-law, Mr. Clement leaves his bag with his beautiful wife, and heads into the travel shop a few yards away, where he grabs bottled waters, energy drinks, pretzels, granola bars, Starburst, M&Ms, and a coloring book, for when his daughter, Sophie, wakes up.

He is in line to pay, certain he has plenty of time to rejoin his family in line, when his phone vibrates against his hip. He fumbles with his purchases, cradling them in one arm so he can pull the phone out of his pocket to see the name on the display.

It is a familiar one.

I blink, not able to make sense of seeing my father's name on my screen. I had already slipped into Mr. Clement's skin and was looking forward to a peaceful flight with my family to Frankfurt, Germany. I don't intend to answer the call, but for some reason I find myself tapping the green button and putting the phone to my ear.

"What can I do for you?" I ask in a pleasant voice, determined not to give my father the satisfaction of knowing how much he's hurt me. All the hurt is almost over. As soon as I get on that plane, there is nothing but a bright future with a beautiful, strong, sexy woman, who loves me, exactly the way I am.

"Where are you?" Dad asks, not bothering to hide his irritation. "You need to come home, your mother's worried."

"I bet she is." I smile at the clerk behind the counter as he rings up my purchases. "Mom hates it when things don't go according to plan. And you two really put a lot into this one, didn't you? Quite the investment of time, money, and deception."

My father sighs. "You've made contact

with Caitlin."

"You could say that." I pass over two twenty dollar bills, the clerk hands me back a few coins, and I claim my bag of goodies before starting back to the boarding line.

"Just know that you have to take everything that girl says with a grain of salt, son," my father says in his best litigator voice. "She's an accomplished liar. She pulled the wool over all of our eyes last summer. But as soon as you went into the hospital, we saw her true colors. All she wanted was money, and she was willing to do anything to get it. She tried to blackmail me and your mother and—"

"Oh please, Dad," I say with a laugh, stopping next to a row of wall phones no one is using, to watch the boarding line creep forward, not wanting to get close enough for Caitlin or the kids to overhear my conversation. "I don't know which is more impressive, the number of lies in that sentence, or the number of idioms. I thought you were supposed to be an award-winning orator. Seriously, I'm embarrassed for you."

"Gabriel, you need to be very careful," Aaron says, his irritation with me coming through loud and clear. "Things are going to be put into motion tomorrow that, once they're started, can't be stopped. If you want to avoid going to jail with that girl, you need to come home right now, and have a long talk with me and your mother about how we move forward from here."

I hum beneath my breath, lifting a hand to Caitlin when she turns to look for me. She hitches Emmie higher in her arms and lifts her brows. I hold up one finger and she smiles, and it is the most beautiful thing I've ever seen. Because there is nothing but truth in that smile, nothing but heart and hope. I know what real love feels like now, and nothing my father can say can destroy what Caitlin and I have rediscovered.

All the money and power and influence in the world can't hold a candle to the power of this kind of love.

"Did you hear me, son?" my father asks. "It's time to get your life back on track before it's too late. You have a legacy to live up to. I don't want you to pay the price for falling in with the wrong kind of girl, but if you give me no other choice…"

"There's always a choice, Dad," I say. "You had a choice whether or not to defend people you knew were guilty. You had a choice whether to try to bully me into being exactly like you for my entire childhood."

"Now, see here, Gabriel, I—"

"And you had a choice whether or not to trick me into having the surgery, and then lie to me about Caitlin after," I say, judging by the stunned silence that Aaron is surprised to learn I've recovered that particular memory. "But even though I want to hate you for telling Caitlin I was dead, and breaking her heart, I can't. Because without you, I wouldn't have had the surgery, or be here with Caitlin right now. I have a second chance at life with the woman I love because of you, Dad, so I want to say…thank you. Thank you, and enjoy the rest of your life. I hope you can forget you ever had a son who caused you so much trouble."

I hang up before he can answer, and move to tuck my phone back into my pocket, but at the last minute I toss it into the trash can along with the receipt from my purchases. I join Caitlin and the kids in line and take my backpack from Ray, who shoots my paper bag an interested look.

"Any candy in there, Gabe?" Ray asks.

"Starburst and M&Ms," I say, laughing when his eyes light up. "But you have to ask Caitlin when it's okay to have them."

"As soon as we find our seats and get buckled in," Caitlin says, smiling at Ray. "I think we all deserve a treat."

"I want M&Ms before my pretzels," Sean says, looking more awake than he did a few minutes ago, clearly excited by the beginning of our adventure. "No, I want M&Ms *and* pretzels at the same time!"

"Gross," Ray says, wrinkling his nose.

"It's not gross," Sean protests in a louder voice. "It's delicious."

"Hush guys, you'll wake Emmie," Caitlin says, glancing up at me as we shuffle a few steps closer to the front of the line. "Everything okay?"

I nod. "Just saying goodbye. Looks like we were smart to leave tonight."

Her eyes widen. "Your parents?"

"My dad," I said. "But it's okay. He didn't have any idea where we were. We'll be gone before he figures out where we've gone."

Caitlin nods, her brows drawing together. "How about you, are you okay?"

"I'm perfect." I put my arm around her shoulders, and draw her close to my side for the rest of our shuffle to the front of the line. We separate long enough to give the stewardess our tickets, but come back together as we walk down the jet way. We sit together on the flight, with Emmie sprawled across our laps, and Caitlin falls asleep on my shoulder just after the movie.

But I stay awake, watching her sleep, too high to close my eyes. I'm high on escape, and on anticipation for our life ahead. But most of all, I'm high on the love I feel for this woman I am lucky enough to call mine. No matter what the future holds, or how many lies we'll have to tell to protect ourselves from the past, I know one thing will always be true—loving Caitlin is the greatest rush I'll ever know.

epilogue

Caitlin

Seven summers later

"How do I love thee? Let me count the ways."
-Elizabeth Barrett Browning

W e arrive at the summer cottage the same time we do every year, just after the spring chill has faded from the air, but the sea is still too cold to swim in, while the village of Porec is still relatively tourist free, and the only bustle on the streets is from the fisherman heading out to sea in the early morning light.

I always get up early the first few days of the trip to sit on the porch with a cup of tea and watch the ships drift out toward the horizon, savoring the moments of peace before the chaos of the day begins. It's something I've done since that first summer, when we came here fresh from that miserable year that is a dim memory now, but this is the first time Danny has joined me in my early morning ritual.

My brother, like most twenty-year-olds, isn't big on getting up before sunrise.

"You're sure you're going to be okay?" he asks, tucking his sandy blond hair behind his ears. It's long enough to tie back, but still tangled from sleep at five-thirty in the morning. "You don't need me to stay a little longer?"

I smile. "I'm fine. Gabe already has Emmie enrolled in dance lessons three days a week, and Ray has his job at the bookstore to keep him busy. We'll just have to find a way to keep Sean entertained until his friends from school come down in a few weeks, but everything else is under control."

Danny's eyes drop pointedly to my swollen belly. "But what about You Know Who?" he asks, our nickname for the unborn baby.

Gabe and I decided we didn't want to know the sex until our son or daughter was born, which resulted in my brothers coming up with all kinds of nicknames for the baby including Critter, Loin Fruit Number One, and Creature from the Womb Lagoon. Needless to say, I'm glad "You Know Who" is the name that stuck.

"The baby is fine. We're both doing great, and Gabe is hovering enough for three fathers," I say. "Go have a great summer with Sam."

"Did I hear my name?" Gabe steps out onto the porch, coffee in hand. He's wearing striped pajama pants, and a battered gray tee shirt, with his hair sticking up in ten different directions, and sleep puffing the edges of his bright blue eyes, but he still takes my breath away.

The man keeps getting better looking—or I keep falling deeper in love with him, one or the other. Either way, just looking at him is still enough to make me feel lit up from the inside out.

"Caitlin said you were cramping her pregnant lady style," Danny says, grinning that wicked grin I would say he inherited from Gabe if they were related by blood.

"I did not." I shift over on the porch swing to make room for my husband. He sits, and I swing my legs into his lap, knowing I'll get a foot rub as soon as he finishes his coffee. "I said you were very…attentive."

Gabe lifts a skeptical brow. "Well, the baby will be born soon, and then I can hover around her crib, instead. Give you your space."

I shake my head, lips curving. "You know I don't want my space." I lean in for a kiss and Danny groans.

"Could you please give it a rest, you two?" he asks. "Some of us haven't seen our girlfriends since Christmas. It's not fair to rub your love in everyone's face."

"Don't be jealous," Gabe mumbles against my lips as he kisses me again. "She has terrible morning breath."

I pull back with a laugh and slap his arm, careful not to spill my tea. "I do not, you rat. I brushed my teeth before I came outside."

Gabe grins as he sets his coffee on the table beside the swing, brings his coffee-cup-warmed hands to my puffy ankles, and begins to rub. "Just trying to ease Danny's pain, *draga*." Out of all of us, Gabe has assimilated to our new country the best. We all speak Croatian now, but Gabe is the only one who uses Croatian pet names.

We probably could have gone back to the states several years ago—Gabe's parents never did turn over that tape, and no charges were filed against me—but we liked our new home even more than we thought we would.

It felt good to start over in a place with history, and a weight to it neither of us had ever felt in South Carolina. We all ditched our fake personas a few months into our adventure—a relief for everyone, especially the kids, who had a hard time getting used to their new names—and Gabe and I applied for citizenship. We have decided to stay in Croatia indefinitely, though Emmie and the boys are still citizens of the United States.

"So have you gotten hold of Sam?" Gabe asks, his nimble fingers working their magic on my aching feet. I never dreamed being eight months pregnant would be so hard on my ankles, but they hurt even worse than the small of my back.

Danny shakes his head, and the smile fades from his face. "No. But I'm sure she's just busy with finals and other college girl stuff."

"I'm sure she'll call soon," I say, hoping I'm right.

Miraculously, Danny and Sam have stayed together for seven years, maintaining their relationship long distance during the school year, and meeting up on Maui every summer, when Sam goes to visit her mother, and Danny goes to stay with Sherry and Bjorn.

Their relationship has lasted longer than a lot of adult marriages. It would be sad to see them break up now, when Sam is halfway through college, and Danny is making enough money as a videographer and extreme sports tour guide to set them up with a nice little nest egg by the time Sam graduates.

Danny shrugs. "Yeah. I'm sure she will." But he doesn't sound sure, and I can tell his light, teasing mood is gone for the day. "I'll go finish packing, then. If you're sure you don't need me hanging around."

"We'll get by, even though we'll miss you," I say, smiling at this tall, muscular man my little brother has somehow become. "Wake Emmie up when you go in, okay? She wants to come with you and Gabe to the airport to say goodbye, and you know it takes an hour for her to get her butt out of bed."

Danny laughs. "She's such a slug. I never got to sleep late in the summer when I was eleven. You had me up making breakfast for everyone by seven every day."

"Poor thing," I say with mock pity. "But look what a good man you grew up to be, in spite of your summers filled with pain and suffering."

"Right, right," Danny says, chuckling as he disappears into the house.

Gabe and I are quiet for a long time after, sitting in companionable silence as the air grows lighter and the ocean sparkles in the first rays of sunlight creeping over the mountains. We watch the water until the fishermen's boats are specks on the horizon and the only movement is the gentle roll of the waves toward shore.

"What are you thinking?" Gabe finally asks, hands still busy on my grateful feet.

"I don't know. I'm a little sad, I guess, knowing Danny isn't coming back from Maui this time. It feels like his life with us is really over."

"It's not over," Gabe says. "He knows he'll always have a home here."

I nod, fighting a wave of emotion, refusing to cry before eight o'clock in the morning, no matter how many pregnancy hormones are coursing through my body. "I know. And he's a pain in my ass. I should be glad he's finally leaving the nest, right?"

Gabe presses a kiss to my forehead. "I love your good heart."

"I love your good fingers," I say, wiggling my toes. "Do I still get foot rubs after You Know Who is born?"

"Of course." He leans in for another kiss. "I mean, I plan on getting you knocked up again as soon as possible, so…"

"No way." I smile so hard our teeth bump together through our lips. "I want at least two years between babies. No Irish twins for this Irish girl."

"All right," he says, nipping at my bottom lip. "As long as you promise I'll get lots of practice time in the bedroom. I don't want to forget how to make babies while we're waiting for number two."

I sigh into his mouth, my skin tingling at the thought. "Sounds like a plan."

We kiss for a long, sweet moment and pull away with twin hums of contentment, and just like that, I'm not worried about Danny leaving any more. My brother will be okay. He has a family who loves him, and even if things with Sam don't work out, he'll always have us. He'll always have a home with me, Gabe, Ray, Sean, Emmie, and You Know Who.

A home full of laughter and love, where it's okay to make mistakes, and color outside the lines.

Speaking of…

"So how did the job go last night?" I ask Gabe, licking his coffee taste from my lips.

"Perfect," he says. "In and out in ten minutes and, thanks to a virus unleashed on his computer, Mr. Anic will have a much more difficult time stealing tourists' credit card information this season."

I smile, but I can't help feeling a little jealous. "I want to be busy. I don't like sitting on the sidelines."

"You've been helping set up a daycare, taking Emmie to a million lessons, and cooking a baby. You've hardly been sitting on the sidelines."

I scrunch my nose and shrug. "Yeah, but you know what I mean."

Gabe and I are more selective about our targets, and more cautious than we used to be, but tipping the scales of justice back in favor of the underdog is still one of our favorite hobbies.

Gabe squeezes my foot. "It won't be much longer now. And just think how much babysitting Sean is going to owe us in exchange for letting his obnoxious friends stay here for an entire month."

I laugh. "All sixteen year olds are obnoxious. They can't help it. But you're right. He's going to have to pay for our pain and suffering. And babysitting will be good for him. I think helping take care of Emmie when she was little made Danny and Ray more empathetic people."

"And less inclined to accidentally get a girl

pregnant," Gabe says, making me laugh.

"True," I say. "Changing a few, poop-up-the-back diapers will do that."

Gabe's brows lift. "Is that a real thing?"

I grin, launching into an in-depth description of the time I had to cut Emmie's onesie off of her body to keep from getting the poo that had squirted up to her neck into her hair, laughing as Gabe plays up trying not to gag.

I laugh so loud that I wake the baby, who gives me a strong kick.

"Ow," I say, still laughing as I smooth my tee-shirt over my belly, glancing down in time to see something small, adorable, and bony ripple the skin of my stomach.

"There's the little alien." Gabe lays his hand on my stomach, an awed expression crossing his face as You Know Who rewards him with another kick. "That…never gets old."

I reach up, patting his scruffy cheek. "Neither do you."

And then he kisses me, and it is better than our first kiss, or our hundredth, or our thousandth, because every day we spend together proves that some things just keep getting better.

Like wine, and cheese, and a love like the

one I was lucky enough to find one hot Carolina summer.

The End

Craving more Cooney family romantic
suspense?
Fall in love with Danny and Sam
in Run With Me
Available Now.

Keep reading for a free sneak peek of
Run with Me.

Sneak Peek
of RUN WITH ME
by Jessie Evans w/a
Lili Valente

About the Book

Warning: A red hot, gut-wrenching, rip-your-heart out read.

When you're going through hell… *Run.*

When I met Samantha Collins, I was a juvenile delinquent on the road to being a violent piece of shit like the rest of the men in my family. But falling for Sam changed all that.

Loving Sam is what I'm good at, what I'm made for. Nothing matters the way she matters.

So when she wants to run away with me for the summer, I don't hesitate. Who wouldn't want to spend three months on a sexy adventure with his favorite person?

But soon it hits me—Sam isn't running away with me. She's running from something else, something dark and ugly that will rip our world apart.

CLIFFHANGER ALERT: Run With Me is a full-length novel that ends in a cliffhanger.

Fight for You, Book Two, the conclusion to Danny and Sam's story, is available now.

Chapter One

Present Day

Samantha

*"And thus the heart will break,
yet brokenly live on."*
-Lord Byron

We're not going to make it.

We're not going to fucking make it.

I pace back and forth across the flowered carpet in front of Gate 11B, fighting the urge to scream as the minutes tick by and the Croatia based flight crew takes their sweet time getting the doors to the Jetway open.

Danny is less than fifty feet away, but he might as well be at ten thousand feet. I can't get to him, he can't get out, and we're about ten minutes from missing our last chance to get out of Maui before it's too late.

The plane to Auckland, New Zealand leaves in twenty-five minutes. They've almost finished boarding. Every time my pacing takes me closer to Gate 7, I can see the line of people shuffling past the flight attendant dwindling.

Twelve people…nine…seven…

I squeeze my fingers into a fist and press it hard to my lips, afraid I might actually scream in the middle of the international terminal if I don't.

Panic dumps into my bloodstream and for a moment all I can hear is the blood rushing in my ears and the desperate *thud thud thud* of my heart thrashing in my chest. My ribs contract, my lungs seize up, and the urge to run becomes almost unbearable.

Dad and Penelope think I'm just picking up Danny at the airport, but if Alec calls while I'm gone they might start to suspect something. If they take a second to glance in my closet, they'll know I've packed for an epic journey, not a forty-minute drive to Kahului. They could come looking for me, force me to go home with them tonight, and put me on a plane back to California tomorrow.

My stepbrother's future hangs in the balance. Penny never believed he was guilty and she'll do anything to prove it, even feed me to the wolves. Penny loves me, but not as much as she loves her son. Not even seven years of being the best and brightest blended family on the island can change that.

I glance at my watch. It's three thirty in Los Angeles. Two hours past my one-thirty appointment time with Detective Spanuth. I'm betting Alec knows I've missed it by now, and I know he wasn't kidding when he said he'd tell our parents the truth if I didn't come clean about the subpoena and everything else.

I don't think he's called his mom yet, but it's only a matter of time. He needed me to keep that meeting, and prove he isn't responsible for what happened to Deidre Jones. If the police believe my version of events, Alec's buddies might still go to jail, but Alec believes unveiling my secret is going to make everything all right. He thinks, once the beans are spilled, the lawyers will be able to prove this was all some big misunderstanding, and the boys are blameless.

I'm the one who started the rumor, after all. I'm the one who hurt that girl.

Innocent girl, whose only sin was looking too much like me.

I close my eyes, swallow hard against the nausea making my stomach heave, and force Deidre's face from my mind. If I could go back in time and take it back, I'd like to believe I would. I'd like to believe I'd do the right thing, but if I look deep into my heart…

My heart….

I'm not sure I have a heart anymore. It feels like there's nothing at the core of me except fear, pain, and hate. I hate Alec and his friends and I hate myself. And when a person is this full of hate, maybe there's no room for anything else.

When I booked this trip late last night— hiding under the covers in my room like I was a ten year old reading after lights out—I was certain all I needed was distance to make everything all right. Just distance and Danny, and I could be the person I used to be. I could put the past five months behind me and move on.

I am rotting from the inside, hanging on to my sanity by a fraying thread, and so sad it feels like I'll never smile a real smile again, but Danny always knows what to say to talk me back from the edge. In his arms, with his love wrapped around me, muffling the chaos of the world, I was sure I'd be able to feel good again.

Or at least okay.

But maybe I was wrong. Maybe this time I'm too broken for anyone to put the pieces back together again.

No sooner is the thought through my head than the door to the Jetway opens. Two businessmen in rumpled suits are the first out, then a family with a little girl asleep in her father's arms. Danny is right behind them, his familiar overstuffed North Face backpack dangling from one hand.

His long, dark blond hair is pulled back in a tangled ponytail, his green eyes look bruised from lack of sleep, and he has his patchy, golden version of five o'clock shadow, but I've never seen anyone more beautiful than he is to me at this moment. The second our eyes meet and he smiles that crooked grin, I know it's not too late. It's not too late for me, and it's not too late for Danny and me to have the fresh start I've been praying for since I woke up New Year's Day.

I still love him. I love him so much that, by the time he crosses the carpet in three long steps and scoops me up in one strong arm, tears of relief are streaming down my face.

"Thank God," I mumble against his neck. He smells so good. So safe.

"Damn, I'm glad you're here. I've missed you so much," he whispers into my hair, hugging me so tight my feet leave the floor and my breasts flatten against his thickly muscled chest.

By the time we were seventeen, Danny had five inches on me, but it's only in the past two years that he's become the kind of man whose chest turns heads when we walk down the beach. If someone had told me when I was thirteen and still capable of pinning Danny to the sand when we wrestled that one day he would have fifty pounds of pure muscle on me, I would have laughed.

When we first started dating, Danny and I were both five-three and I outweighed him by ten pounds, no matter how vehemently he insisted he weighed in at one forty. He was the runt of our junior high school, even shorter and skinnier than the two genius kids who'd skipped a grade.

But he isn't a runt anymore. Working as an extreme-sports tour guide has made him strong, strong enough to hold me in one arm and his giant backpack in the other. Hopefully, strong enough to slay the demons that have kept me awake for forty-eight hours as I ran from the nightmare my life in Los Angeles has become. If we can just get on that plane and on our way to the opposite hemisphere, everything might still be all right.

"Come on," I say, pressing a swift kiss to his scruffy cheek before pushing on his chest.

"We've got to hurry, or we'll miss our flight."

His eyebrows lift as he sets me down. "Where are we going?"

"New Zealand." I take his hand and pull him toward the gate, feeling like my heart is going to explode with relief when I see the door to the Jetway still open. "I've booked rooms for our first four days," I say over my shoulder. "After that, we'll see where the adventure takes us."

"I thought we had to wait until after you graduated," Danny says, even as he picks up his pace, hurrying toward Gate 7 beside me. "Did your dad change his mind?"

"No, *I* changed my mind," I say. "I have some savings and I decided it was past time to use it."

"Sam, wait." Danny slows and his hand squirms free of mine. "I can't let you do this. The tickets must have cost thousands of dollars, and I told you, I'm cash poor until the business—"

"I don't care," I say, snatching his hand and holding on tight. "You can pay me back later. Or never, I don't care. I just need to do this.

Now. With you."

"Why?" His tired eyes narrow as he searches my face. "What's going on Sam? Why haven't you returned my calls? I swear, I was starting to think…"

"Thinking is overrated," I say, throat tightening as panic threatens to take over again. We have to get on that plane. Only when we're strapped into our seats in row twenty-two will I finally be able to take a breath without feeling like it might be my last.

"I don't know," Danny says, hurt clear in his voice. "I knew you were okay because your dad said he'd talked to you, but I—"

"I'm so sorry." I cut him off before he can say what I know he's thinking. I can't stand to hear him say he thought I was going to end it, or think about how close I came to telling him I never wanted to see him again. "I should have answered the phone, I've just been…really upset."

"I thought I was the person you talked to when you were upset," he says, the furrow between his brows deepening. "Or has something changed?"

"Nothing's changed," I lie, forcing a brittle smile.

I reach up, smoothing away the line between his brows the way I always do, even that simple touch reminding me that we are us. We are Sam and Danny and together we're bigger and stronger than anything chasing me.

We have to be, or I've emptied my savings and flushed my future down the toilet for nothing.

"I've been doing a lot of hard thinking," I continue, holding his troubled gaze. "About college and my family and all the compromises I've made so that other people can be happy…"

I swallow past the lump rising in my throat. "I'm just so tired of it. I'm tired of waiting for my life to start. That's why I want to go on this trip. With you, my favorite person."

He sighs, "Sam, you know I've been dying to—"

"Passengers Samantha Collins and Daniel Cooney." The female voice on the loudspeaker turns the middle of Danny's last name into an "ew" sound, making him raise an eyebrow. "Please report to gate seven for immediate boarding, the doors are about to close."

"Please!" I capture Danny's hand in both of mine and squeeze. "Please, just get on this plane with me. We can talk about anything you want once we're on board. We'll have ten hours in the air to catch up on everything we've missed since Christmas."

The skin around Danny's eyes relaxes, but the uncertainty in them remains. "I don't know, Sam. Do you really think this is the right time?"

"Yes! Absolutely, yes!" I fight to keep the tears from my eyes. If I start crying again, Danny's going to know something a lot more serious than a missed flight is to blame.

He knows me too well, something I should have considered when I put this crazy plan into motion. We can run halfway around the world, but if I can't leave the past behind, it won't matter how far I am from the scene of the crime. Danny will know something's wrong, and he'll get to the truth, sooner or later. The past few months have proven I can hold up under incredible amounts of stress, but I've never been able to hold up under the gentle weight of his eyes.

Danny shakes his head. "After this week, and the way you've been on the phone the past few months…"

He bites his lip for a moment before pushing on. "Things don't feel the same, and it's more than the time or distance. It feels like you're hiding something from me."

I'm hiding everything.

I'm hiding a secret so ugly it could destroy every dream we've had since we were too young to realize how lucky we were to have found each other.

Or how hard it would be to keep love alive in a world like this one.

Aloud, I say, "We don't have time for the No Bullshit game, but I promise you, if you get on that plane, you won't be sorry. I'll make you remember why you fell in love with me, Danny, I promise."

"You don't have to remind me." He reaches out with both hands, squeezing my arms below the capped sleeves of my gray tee shirt. "I still love you so much." He pulls in a rough breath and continues in a softer voice, "I just need to know you still love me."

"I do." I fight the tears pushing at the backs of my eyes. "And I don't want to lose you, okay? I can't lose you."

"You're not going to lose me," he says. "Come on, Sam. You know me. I'm with you. For keeps."

"Then come with me." I cup his scruffy cheeks and stand on tiptoe, bringing our faces closer together. "Let's have that adventure we've been dreaming about forever."

Before he can respond, I press my lips to his.

It's our first kiss since Christmas, and my first kiss since my life started falling apart. I don't expect to feel anything—I'm so desperate to get on the plane I'm certain there's no room on my neural pathways for anything but panic—but the moment his warm lips brush mine, something deep inside me flutters.

Nearly forgotten wings beat, sending dust puffing into the air, reminding me that there is still life in the locked rooms of my heart. Parts of me have been covered with blankets and secreted away, but they haven't been destroyed. With Danny's help, there might be hope for me yet, and even the possibility of hope is enough to make me get down on my knees and beg him to run away with me if that's the only way to convince him.

But thankfully, it seems a kiss—and hearing our names called over the loudspeaker again, this time accompanied by the warning that this would be our "final call"—is all it takes to win Danny over.

"Okay," he says, threading his fingers through mine. "But I'll probably have the world's worst case of jet lag by the time we get there."

"It's okay." My heart lifts as we hurry toward the gate. "I booked a room near the airport for our first night. We can crash as soon as we get there. Just draw the curtains and sleep for twenty-four hours straight if we need to."

He groans. "That sounds like heaven. I didn't sleep at all on the last flight. The guy next to me was snoring loud enough to shake the entire row of seats."

"You can sleep in my lap if you want." I hand our tickets to the agent at the gate, a sour-faced woman who looks out of place in the cheery Hawaiian Airlines uniform. "I'm too wired to sleep."

"I don't want to sleep yet," Danny says. "We should talk first."

"All the overhead bins are full," the agent says, casting a pointed look at Danny's giant weathered backpack, distracting from the anxious look I'm sure just flickered across my face. "You're going to have to check that at the end of the Jetway."

While Danny fills out the bright orange luggage tag and gets it strapped to his pack, I give myself a mental pep talk worthy of my toughest volleyball coach back in high school. It's time to leave all the shit in the locker room and get out onto the court.

If I carry my misery and pain onto the plane, I'm going to ruin my new life before it gets started. There's no room for that junk in my head anymore. I'm going to leave it right here, at the door to the Jetway, a pile of psychic waste I'm better off without. Regret isn't going to change the past, and I can't survive for much longer carrying the weight of two ruined lives on my shoulders.

It may make me a bad person or a sociopath or something worse, but I'm officially erasing the past five months—and anyone or anything that reminds me of them—from my timeline. From here on out, it's Danny and me against the world and I will do whatever I have to do to protect our second chance.

Our *last* chance, because if this fails, I know there won't be enough of me left to try again.

"Ready?" Danny shoulders his pack and turns to me with a smile.

"Ready." I take his hand and follow him down the Jetway without a single look back over my shoulder.

I'm leaving the past behind and I swear on everything good in the world that I will never, ever look back.

RUN WITH ME
Is Available Now

Acknowledgements

First and foremost, thank you to my readers. Every email and post on my Facebook page have meant so much. I can't express how deeply grateful I am for the chance to entertain you.

More big thanks to my Street Team, who I am convinced are the sweetest, funniest, kindest group of people around. You inspire me and keep me going and I'm not sure I'd be one-third as productive without you. Big tackle hugs to all.

More thanks to the Facebook groups who have welcomed me in, to the bloggers who have taken a chance on a newbie, and to everyone who has taken time out of their day to write and post a review.

And of course, many thanks to my husband, who not only loves me well but also supports me in everything I do. I don't know how I got so lucky, man, but I am hanging on tight to you.

Tell Lili your favorite part!

I love reading your thoughts about the books and your review matters. Reviews help readers find new-to-them authors to enjoy. So if you could take a moment to leave a review letting me know your favorite part of the story—nothing fancy required, even a sentence or two would be wonderful—I would be deeply grateful.

About the Author

Lili Valente has slept under the stars in Greece, eaten dinner at midnight with French men who couldn't be trusted to keep their mouths on their food, and walked alone through Munich's red light district after dark and lived to tell the tale.

These days you can find her writing in a tent beside the sea, drinking coconut water and thinking delightfully dirty thoughts.

Lili loves to hear from her readers. You can reach her via email at
lili.valente.romance@gmail.com
or like her page on Facebook
https://www.facebook.com/AuthorLiliValente?ref=hl

You can also visit her website:
http://www.lilivalente.com/

Also By Lili Valente

Sexy Flirty Dirty Series:
Magnificent Bastard (A Sexy Standalone
Romantic Comedy)
Spectacular Rascal (A Sexy Standalone
Romantic Comedy)
Miraculous Mess (October 2016)

The Under His Command Series:
Controlling Her Pleasure
Commanding Her Trust
Claiming Her Heart

The Bought by the Billionaire Series:
Dark Domination
Deep Domination
Desperate Domination
Divine Domination

**The Kidnapped by the Billionaire
Series:**
Dirty Twisted Love
Filthy Wicked Love

CPSIA information can be obtained
at www.ICGtesting.com
Printed in the USA
FSHW010854230619
59335FS